D1189122

ESCAPE FROM THE PAST

Driving northward in the hope of leaving behind her old life and painful memories, Clare Bowers takes a wrong turn in the mist and ends up in a ditch, from which she is rescued and taken to stay at Moorlands Farm. The owners have had their own tragedies in the past, and there is still a bitter feud between them and the Laytons at the nearby farm. Then Clare meets the darkly handsome Richard Layton, and her past threatens to overtake her again . . .

Books by Iris Weigh
in the Linford Romance Library:

STRANGER AT THE DOOR
HARMONY FOR TWO

IRIS WEIGH

ESCAPE FROM THE PAST

Complete and Unabridged

LINFORD
Leicester

First published in Great Britain in 1975 by
Robert Hale & Company
London

First Linford Edition
published 2014
by arrangement with
Robert Hale Limited
London

A catalogue record for this book is available
from the British Library.

ISBN 978–1–4448–1975–5

Published by
F. A. Thorpe (Publishing)
Anstey, Leicestershire

Set by Words & Graphics Ltd.
Anstey, Leicestershire
Printed and bound in Great Britain by
T. J. International Ltd., Padstow, Cornwall

This book is printed on acid-free paper

For my Cousins,
GWEN and GRACE

1

'Where on earth am I?' Clare peered through the windscreen of her little car at the narrow twisting road ahead. She seemed to have been driving an hour over deserted tawny moorlands and had suddenly plunged down this thickly hedged lane. Yet how could one get lost on the Yorkshire moors? The approaching evening with a hovering mist did not help matters, and possibly after the last village where she had asked directions she must have taken the wrong turning after all.

If this went on she would have to park the car and spend the night there — as soon as she reached a wide space somewhere. At least she felt she had covered her tracks well. No one would find her again, as to all intents and purposes she had gone abroad, wiping the soil of England off her feet for ever.

Perhaps she would at a later date, but in the despairing mood she had been in, weary of everybody and everything, she was not ready for the strangeness and bustle of foreign places. Mrs. Staines, Uncle Ronald's stupid, cloying old nurse, had seen her passport and labels, plans lying about for departure far afield, noticing that she had parted with her car. She would spread the news with glee that at last that was the end of Ronald's niece. She would dig her heels in at the house and live happily on the handsome legacy Ronald had left her.

'But what do I care?' Clare said aloud. 'I'm free at last — to go where I like. I'll never see hateful Mrs. Staines again. Even lost on the moors is preferable to that.'

She had taken a taxi to Dover — because they knew she hated flying — then changed to another taxi, and in the Midlands picked up her car where she had left it and drove at reckless speed northwards. At first she had Scotland in her mind, as far as she could get, John-o-Groats, or even the Orkneys or somewhere, yet here she was lost in a mist on the Yorkshire moors!

Suddenly a bulky form came out of the dimness, lurching towards her, blocking the lane. She spun the wheel sharply and ended up with the bonnet diving into the thorny hedge. She was thrown forward, smacking her head against something heavily and forgot where she was for a short time.

She came around to the sound of voices and strong arms pulling her out of the car. Blinking, she was aware of two or three burly men and a horse and cart.

'Are you all right now, miss?' said one of them with black hair and moustache, bending over her.

'I think so,' she said, holding on to him as he set her on her feet. 'I feel a bit dizzy yet, though, and my head aches.'

'We'll take her up to the farm,' said the biggest of them all. A broad fellow with a tanned face and gingery moustache, and thick dark-red hair flecked with white.

As they helped her into the cart, she faltered, 'My car — my luggage — '

'They'll be safe enough,' said the same man. He got up beside her and took up the reins. 'Louis is getting your car out of the hedge and he'll bring it up for you. You're in no fit state to drive on.'

A third man was trying to calm down another horse, a spirited tubby animal. Clare stared at it, remembering. 'I nearly ran that horse down.'

'Yes, it was all Tilly's fault. She broke loose. Sorry about that. Now sit quiet. The farm isn't far away.'

He did not speak again on the short jerky journey and Clare closed her eyes, her head throbbing, sickness threatening. As they rattled over cobble-stones and he pulled the horse to a halt, she opened her eyes and saw that they were at the rear of a long, grey-stoned house. There were stables and barns to the right, and somewhere quite near the clucking of poultry.

'Shall I lift you down?' asked the man bluntly.

Clare pulled herself together. 'Oh no, I can manage.'

All the same he gripped her arm in a large hand as she clambered down to the ground, and led her across to an open door and into a stone-floored kitchen. To Clare it seemed a huge place, consisting of over half the ground floor of the house. Modern methods appeared not to have encroached here. Clare felt she had gone back in time somewhere — or maybe the knock on her head had made her stupid . . . Yet the big black kitchen range with a red fire glowing behind bars was old all right, and through a door at the side she glimpsed a long shallow sink and shelves of cooking utensils, with crockery hanging on hooks. There were tall cupboards each side of the cooking-range, and in a creaking rocking-chair a little old man, with crisp white hair and a face like wrinkled brown leather, was dozing. A thick-haired sheepdog lay stretched on the tufted mat.

'Martha, bring a cup o' tea,' called the man, sitting Clare at the end of the long scrubbed table.

'What are you wanting tea at this hour for?' a woman grumbled. She came to the inner door then halted, staring in astonishment at Clare's pale face.

'She's had an accident. Hurry up, Martha, get tea — or would you rather — ' he turned to Clare — 'There's nothing stronger than beer in the house.'

'Tea, please,' Clare said weakly.

Evidently a kettle was kept hissing by the stove, for tea was brought to her almost immediately. The woman bent over her.

'No skin broken but you've got a rare bump there,' she said. 'I'll get you something for that. What happened?'

'All Tilly's fault. This lady went into the hedge to avoid driving the mare

6

down.' The man frowned over at Clare. 'How are you feeling? You'll not be wanting a doctor, I hope. I don't hold with doctors.'

'No, of course not. I'll be all right after a rest — but where can I get for the night? I seem to have lost my way.'

'You must stop here. Plenty of room here. Stay as long as you like.'

Clare looked from his unsmiling face to the woman. She did not look exactly pleased. Her grey-streaked hair was smoothed down into a bun at the back of her head, and her stern features and heavy build well resembled the man. 'Do you take paying guests? If so I'd be pleased to stay a while.'

'We have had stray visitors,' Martha said coldly, 'but we're rather out of the way of things here.'

'Martha will make up a bed for you. I'm Joseph Canning, Miss — '

'Clare Bowers.'

'This is my sister Martha and over there my father, Timothy Canning.'

As Martha went through another

door to the other part of the house, snapping it shut noisily behind her, the little old man snorted and came awake. Keen light-coloured eyes stared at the newcomer.

'What are *you* doing here?' he said ungraciously. 'Are you from Layton's? They're always trying to poke their way in here.'

'Nonsense, Father,' said Joseph quickly.

'Are you from Layton's?'

'She's staying here for a time. She had a car accident.'

'Can't the girl speak for herself? She shouldn't be in a car if she can't drive properly.'

'Tilly is to blame. She broke out again.'

'Ha! Going courting again, then?'

'I think the courting is well over. She's likely to foal before long.'

'Oh!' gasped Clare. 'I'm glad I didn't hurt her.'

'Aye, it was lucky. But nothing keeps that mare in. She kicks down doors and fences when the mood takes her, 'specially in the spring.'

'She's a grand little mare.' The old man tamped tobacco down into a black ancient pipe. 'The only thing with a bit o' spirit in this place.'

'Don't listen to the old man,' said Joseph, rising at the sound of footsteps across the cobbled yard. 'He has nothing to do but moan.'

'Can I help it if my back gives way — '

Timothy Canning mumbled on but he was ignored as the man Louis entered with Clare's two suitcases. He put the car key into her hand.

'It's a natty little car,' he said.

Clare smiled faintly. 'Thank you for bringing it in. Is it all right?'

'Nothing wrong, but a few scratches, no doubt.'

There was a young girl behind Louis, a pretty, timid girl with thick auburn hair to her shoulders. She shrank back behind the others as though the sight of a stranger alarmed her.

'My daughter, Penelope,' said Joseph.

'Come here, Penny,' — but the young girl disappeared somewhere in the evening shadows.

'She's dumb, makes her scared,' said Joseph. 'That is — there was a terrible tragedy five years ago and she hasn't spoken since. But you get off to rest now, Miss Bowers. Here's Martha to take you to your room.'

Clare felt she couldn't get her head down quickly enough. She followed the stern-faced woman into a narrow hall and up a short flight of stairs to a long landing with low-ceilinged bedrooms. Martha took Clare to the end as though she couldn't get her far enough away from them.

'I wouldn't be staying here the night if it had been left to her,' pondered Clare, as she was left alone in a fair-sized room. It had an old-fashioned air with its flowery curtains, brown mats on polished brown linoleum and yellowish ugly furniture. Still, it was all clean and sweet spring air came through the small open window, and the bed linen looked crisp and inviting. She picked up a jar of some cool ointment left for her and smoothed it gently over her forehead and bruises, then swallowed some aspirins and went to bed.

She felt much better the next morning and awoke to a room bright with sunshine, its window evidently facing east. She got up and went to look outside. She found she was overlooking a poultry-run, hens already clucking over some corn recently given them, and beyond that was a meadow with a few cows, and further still green moorlands as far as the eye could see.

'I like it here,' she mused. 'So much open space and clean air. Freedom. I'd like to stay.'

She turned to the mirror and grimaced at the red swelling bruise on her forehead. Pulling on a dressing-wrap she went down the long passage to the bathroom Martha had pointed out last night. It had been installed about twenty years ago, the woman had explained briefly. So it was not exactly modern, but at least the basin and bath were roomy and the taps worked, and there was even hot water. What more did one need?

Refreshed and wearing a clean blouse, Clare went downstairs. The door on the right was open and she saw into the other half of the house, a pleasant sitting-room with several windows, cretonne-covered chairs, highly polished floor and furniture. Then she noticed on one of the window-seats the pretty, dumb girl, watching something outside. She pulled a curtain around her as Clare hesitated by the door, almost disappearing from sight as she had the night before. Clare smiled at her, longing to show friendliness, then turned back through the doorway and went into the kitchen. Though the weather was warm, fire still glowed in the grate, and the elderly man with his pipe was in his rocking-chair as though he had never left it, the sole occupant of the room. The big room was bright and cheerful, there was crockery and food on the table and a smell of bacon in the air.

'Good morning, Mr. Canning,' she said.

''Mornin', miss. Sit you down, Martha'll be in with your breakfast in a minute.' His keen old eyes studied her face.

'I suppose I'm late. My watch had stopped.'

'No matter. Joseph'll be in for a bite soon, anyway. He doesn't bother with much early on. That's a fair bruise you've given yourself!'

Clare laughed. 'Yes, it is, isn't it? Hardly adds to my beauty.'

Martha came in and put a plate of bacon and egg in front of Clare. 'Sorry about the bacon. It's gone hard, I'm afraid I'm a poor cook and I don't recommend the porridge.'

'This will do fine. Thank you very much.' The egg, too, looked hard and overdone but Clare did her best to appear to enjoy it. Apparently Martha was one of those unfortunate people who could never make a success of any sort of cooking, however they tried.

Joseph came in from the yard and looked her over anxiously. 'How do you feel now?'

'Much better, thank you. Not much worse for the incident.'

'Stay as long as you like. After all, we were to blame as the owners of that stupid mare.' He took a plate to the stove, stirred some gluey stuff inside a pan and exclaimed, 'Good lord, Martha, this porridge is like cement! When will you learn to make it properly? After all this time I could do better myself.'

'Then why don't you?' snapped his sister.

Clare took a good look at Joseph Canning as they sat at breakfast. In her dazed state last night all she had been aware of was his large frame and dark-red head. He certainly was a big-made man with large ginger-haired-backed hands,

14

quite good looking in a rugged, florid skinned way. He would be in his late forties, she guessed. His hair was thick with sideburns, his eyebrows strong and jutting over steady grey eyes. Like his sister Martha, it seemed he rarely smiled. They both looked stern and forbidding, discontented with their lot.

He in his turn furtively examined the girl opposite him. Twenty-three? In her early twenties, anyway. A bonny kid with her black hair clipped short to the head and long black lashes with her hazel eyes. Bonny in spite of the disfiguring bruise to one side of her face. A slim, neat little figure. A good while since there had been a comely young wench in their house. No one but grumbling, bitter Martha, complaining old Timothy, and poor little helpless Penny.

'Are you coming to look round the place?' he asked Clare, spreading honey on a thick crust of bread.

'There ain't much to see these days,' put in Timothy. 'Once it was a thriving

15

farm, cattle, pigs, the lot.'

'It's pretty fair, enough for us to manage, and there's the garden and the orchard.' Joseph turned back to Clare. 'Only one or two cows now for our own milk — we lost a lot with foot-and-mouth. Since then we've kept to sheep and we rear one or two horses.'

'You'd like to drop the lot for horses, that I know,' said Timothy. 'You're jealous of Layton's. That's another thing, young miss' — he glared over at Clare — 'you'll keep away from Layton's place while you're here.'

'Whatever is Layton's place?' asked Clare.

'Our nearest neighbours and we hate them,' said the younger man coldly. 'There's been war between us for years. They've taken our land. They steal everything of ours they can get their hands on.'

'So you mind, miss. Keep well away,' said Timothy.

'All that's not allowed, surely. Who

16

are they? Gypsies?'

Joseph gave a sharp laugh. 'No, not that, but the farm has been in the family for years, as ours has, and there's always been bad blood between us. My father, and his father before him. Mostly nowadays the Laytons rear fine horses — racehorses.'

Clare wondered what these people across so many acres of ground from them could be like. What had happened to bring such hatred between the two farms? Out of the corner of her eye she saw Penny at the doorway, but as she turned to smile at her, the girl went back to the hall.

'Penny isn't frightened of me, is she?'

'She's a little scared rabbit, always queer with strangers. She'll get used to you. Give her time.' Joseph shook his head. 'It's a big worry. I feel she's missing a lot. Now, come along and I'll show you around.'

'Where is Tilly this morning?' said Clare, rising from the table with him. 'I'd like to see her.'

'She'll be up the home meadow somewhere.'

Though not a short woman she felt much less beside the big Joseph Canning, trying to keep up with his loping stride across the cobbled yard. They went in and out of barns smelling mostly of oats and corn and other animal foodstuffs in great bins. Places with buckets and spades and other gardening implements, windows wreathed in cobwebs, lanterns hanging from rafters, harness along the walls. Her car stood under a big open barn and she was pleased to see it was little damaged, as their man Louis had said. He was working by the stables, swilling out the floors with strong disinfectant. He was a good-looking fellow of about twenty-six with a saucy grin.

'You look much better this morning, miss,' he said to her.

'Yes, I'm fine now.' She touched her forehead, smiling. 'Just a bit disfigured.'

'Glad it was no worse.'

The farm was all run on rather

18

old-fashioned lines, it seemed to Clare, as they set off towards the nearby fields, a sheepdog called Shane at their heels. They had not moved with the times and, no doubt, being out on the moors like this, miles from anywhere, and no youngsters in the family, it had a lot to do with it. The beautiful, untouched moors rose all about them, rising to a blue-grey sky flecked with tiny white clouds, and in the near distance sheep belonging to this farm. There were a few cattle in a small meadow, and in another three or four horses clustered together, the plump little Tilly contentedly cropping grass beside them. She ambled over towards them and nuzzled Clare's arm.

'After sugar,' said Joseph. 'Penny always brings some. She spoils Tilly.'

'I'd have brought some if I'd known,' said Clare, stroking the sleek brown neck, forgiving the gentle animal for the damage of last evening.

'No matter. The mare gets too much.' They walked back beside a great patch of blackened ground and burnt-out old timber. 'Used to be a barn here. Burnt down, terrific fire.' He kicked at a black wrinkled beam amongst the weeds. 'Nothing worthwhile has ever grown here since.' He suddenly seemed to lose interest. 'Now, if you don't mind, I must get back to work. You'll be all right?'

'Yes, of course. Don't let me waste your time.'

'Layton's place — Hilltops — is over there — ' his voice held a warning note as he pointed.

'What is your farm called?' she asked.

'Moorlands — just Moorlands. Come, Shane — ' he looked at her gravely then turned on his heel. The dog looked up at Clare hesitantly then followed him obediently. Even the dogs had learnt not to cross Joseph, it appeared. Already Clare sensed that he was a bitter man, disappointed with life, a hard man to come up against in a disagreement.

She turned away, obstinately walking in the direction he had pointed out. It was a fresh morning, not much sun, and the air was pleasantly invigorating. She came to a little brook, crystal clear, rippling over a pebbly bed, and she crossed over by two or three large stepping-stones. Presently she came to a rise and found herself looking across at the Laytons' property. It stood high, a long stone house not unlike the Cannings', with buildings clustered about it, left, right and centre. It looked a thriving place with a large fenced paddock holding several horses, and some cattle browsing contentedly. There were people moving busily about and, looking further to the right, she saw one or two horses being ridden at a smart gallop against the grey sky.

What a pity, she thought, to be unfriendly with these nearest neighbours all because of some silly old feud handed down over the years. She sighed and turned away. She had better not upset the Cannings by exploring in that direction on her first day. Again she had that strange craving to stay here. Who would look for her here? No walls hemming her in, people watching her every movement, even her thoughts being examined. Here she could walk for miles, come and go as she liked, make new friends.

Walking back towards the brook she saw Penny there, dabbling her fingers in the water. As the girl started to her feet Clare called, 'Penny, wait for me, will you?'

Penny hesitated then waited, tossing her rich auburn hair from her face. At least she had good hearing which was a great help. Clare wondered how she had come to lose her voice and if nothing could be done for her. Some time she would endeavour to find out what had really happened. She went up to the girl and took her hand gently. What a shame it was! . . . such a lovely face, such a slim pretty figure.

'Don't be frightened of me, Penny. Let's be friends, shall we?'

Penny's blue eyes watched her warily, giving no sign whether her company was welcome or not. She drew her hand away but she stayed at Clare's side as they walked back towards the farm.

'Have you given Tilly some sugar yet?' asked Clare.

The girl's face brightened. She nodded then from a pocket she brought half an apple, and by her expressive movements Clare gathered that the horse had eaten apple, too.

'You gave her some apple, did you, this time?'

Penny nodded. 'So she'll be waiting for the rest of the apple, won't she?' Another nod and a slight smile over the lips. 'Then let's take it to her.'

The little mare pricked up her ears and came leisurely over. Clare watched, smiling, as Tilly took the piece of apple off Penny's outstretched palm and munched with enjoyment. Climbing on the fence Penny stroked the smooth brown head and then the rounded body.

'She's going to have a foal, isn't she?' said Clare softly.

Penny nodded, glancing up quickly with bright eyes.

'Has she had any before?' Another nod. 'How many? One — two — ?'

Clare counted on her fingers. Penny held up three fingers, and Clare was made to understand that this was to be the fourth foal. A strong little horse, indeed!

2

Back at the farmhouse Clare and Penny went into the back kitchen where Martha was working red-faced over a gas-stove, stirring vegetables into what appeared to be a large pan of stew. She gave Penny a basket and sent the girl away.

'Eggs,' she said briefly. 'Penny collects them every day, but sometimes when she goes wandering off she forgets.'

'Let me help you,' said Clare, moving over to the shallow sink where there was a clutter of crockery and cooking utensils. 'It's a lot for one to do. Don't you have any help?' she asked, running hot water from a geyser at the side.

'We had a woman but her man got ill and she left.' Martha watched the other making short work of the clearing-up. 'I'm a rotten housekeeper and a worse cook.' She turned back to the stove. 'You'll not stick it here for long.'

Clare had no answer for that, but she silently felt it would take more than a few badly cooked meals to chase her away from this peaceful hideaway. 'Where is your father?' she asked, seeing the rocking-chair still and empty through the open door.

'He'll be up the garden somewhere. I'm glad to have him out from under my feet for a time.' Martha's hard voice softened slightly. 'He loves gardening but he can't do much. When it's raining and he's kept in he nearly drives me mad.'

'I'll help him while I'm here,' said Clare. 'I like gardening, too.' She paused, then added, 'Martha, if you'll tell me where to find things I'll set the table for you.'

The kitchen livened up with the coming of the four men. Louis, who had a room over a stable, and Dan from the village — two miles away so they said — stayed for their midday dinner.

Penny returned, put her basket of eggs in the back kitchen and slid quietly into a seat beside her father. The stew was greasy with lumps of fat floating about. Clare sorted it out as well as she could, managing to eat some of it and relieved to see that Martha was not watching. After doling out the food Martha lost all interest and picked at a small amount on her own plate. Joseph gave it a look of disgust then ate rapidly with no visible enjoyment, while old Timothy swallowed the lot, evidently used to eating all that lay before him without trouble. But the food was poor and tasteless, the pudding that followed heavy and unappetising, at least to Clare's fastidious taste. Martha was certainly an indifferent cook and apparently had no heart to try improving herself.

'I've been making friends with Penny,' Clare said, looking at the girl's downbent head and the small fingers picking at a portion of the meal with little appetite.

'Have you, then?' Joseph's eyes followed hers and rested on his daughter for a moment. 'She'll get used to you.'

'If she stays long enough,' put in Martha.

'Why shouldn't she stay a while, that is, if she has the time?' said Joseph. 'Where were you heading for, Miss Bowers?'

'Nowhere in particular. I'm at a somewhat loose end.'

'Well, there's nothing much here for you.' Martha began to pile the plates together.

'You're welcome as long as you want, anyway,' said her brother. 'Take no notice of Martha.'

Clare stared at the solemn-faced woman. Didn't she want her — or any stranger — there? Perhaps she simply thought it meant more work, more cooking which she seemed to dislike so much.

Yet in spite of the solid, untempting food Clare enjoyed the days following.

There was something charming and restful about the long stone house, practically unchanged since it was built for one of the hard-working Cannings many years ago. Once or twice she had taken her car out of the open barn and driven down to the village, Lambreck. The little old place had hardly altered, either, over the years, with its white row of cottages and tiny post-office.

She spent a good deal of her time in the garden. It was overgrown and tangled, neglected, because most of the others spent all their energy with the animals and in the fields. Penny seemed attracted to her, but achieving her full friendship was slow. The girl was apt to shy away from any advances like a timid colt. Martha, too, was dour and secretive, accepting Clare's help with ironing and mending, or in the kitchen, with no sign of gratitude.

One day, however, she broke into a string of curses as she burnt herself at the oven. 'This damn family!' she groaned. 'I shouldn't be stuck here at the stove. My place is with the animals. It always was in the past.' She almost flung the dish of overdone food on to the big table that was scratched and furrowed with the years. 'Just look at that! Joseph would be more use in the kitchen than I am. I'm at home in the stables, on the land in the open air.'

It was as though all her longings and feelings had been bottled up so long they had to burst out at last. She crossed to the window and flung it wide open, craving the fresh moorland air outside.

'You can only do your best,' said Clare cautiously.

'I loathe it, Miss Bowers. If only Joe would marry again and let me go free.'

'You've never thought of leaving here? Breaking away?'

'I couldn't, could I? Not unless Joe took a wife. There's the old man and poor little Penny. However much I hate it I couldn't desert those two. We haven't been able to find a woman to help in Harriet's place. It's difficult finding anyone to live out here these days.'

For the first time Clare felt sorry for the hard-faced woman, for she knew herself how bitter life could be. Martha was of the same stamp as her brother, a tough, outdoor type. At least, thought Clare, I can lighten the load for her a little while I am here. Still, as so often happened, at the mid-day meal, Joseph poked discontentedly at his plate of food.

'Good heavens, Martha, when are you ever going to learn to cook? Whatever you do turns out a mess.'

'I've only one answer — if you can do better, you're welcome,' retorted Martha.

'Ever since Harriet went it's been murder.' As Clare started, he glanced at her with a wry smile. 'Pardon, Miss Bowers, but it makes me so angry, and with you here — a guest — how can she put such food in front of you?' He jabbed again at his plate. 'A great pity Harriet had to leave, but her ailing husband needed her.'

Clare felt there was a quarrel brewing. Martha's brow was lowering, her lips tight, and probably only Clare's presence restrained her.

'Martha was never a house-woman like her ma,' put in Timothy. 'Lydia tried to train her but it were no use. Always the animals with the lass.'

'There were plenty of animals then, too,' said Martha acidly. 'Perhaps if you'd left me there we'd have kept up a place like Layton's. Instead of going to rot and ruin — '

'We need men. Louis and Dan do as much as they can,' said Joseph.

Looking up Clare met Louis's dark eyes across the table. There was a gleam of mischief in them. He was enjoying this not unusual fracas between brother and sister.

'Aye, we need men,' said Timothy. 'There's men over yon, sons working with their fathers. All Joseph could breed was wenches and a lad with no sinews for the farm — four of 'em

— and where are they?'

'You didn't do so fine yourself,' said Joseph. 'So shut up, Father.'

'Aye, nine and all under the earth but Joe and Martha here and two others married and the Lord knows where. There's always an answer to it, Joe. If you had sense you'd get yourself a woman again. Five years a widower — '

'I can get a woman whenever I want.'

'If that Walters woman had her wits about her — '

'It suits me as it is, so shut up, Father,' Joseph said again. He turned away and finished his meal quickly with hunger but no enjoyment.

'I have a suggestion to make,' broke in Clare, with sudden inspiration. 'I would like to stay here for some time and if you'll allow me, in return, I'll cook for you and leave Martha free for the house and other things. There's no question of salary. I'd just like to stay and I enjoy cooking.'

She halted, flushing. What had possessed her? Yet she was sorry for

Martha — and for Penny. They grumbled and swore before her, so why should she worry about politeness? Joseph pushed his plate away, apparently speechless for a moment, and stared across at his sister. Her face had changed from amazement to eagerness, waiting for him to speak. In that short minute Clare realised that his word was law in that house, even riding over his complaining old father. Timothy left the table and went to his rocking-chair.

'We could do with the help,' he said, scraping at his ancient pipe.

'I am a good cook, I promise you,' said Clare quietly. 'In return all I need is board and lodging for some time.'

Joseph looked from Martha to Clare. 'It sounds like a good idea. Thank you, Miss Bowers.'

'All of you please call me Clare. It would seem more like home. If you will tell me what you'd like to eat, Mr. Canning?'

'Joseph, yes? I eat anything if it is not a block of cement.'

'Stop getting at me, Joe,' sighed Martha.

'Leave Martha alone,' said Timothy, with brief amiability. 'She does her best and it ain't been easy for her.'

'It will be nice for Penny, too, to have you here,' said Joseph. 'It is a poor life for her.'

Penny had been listening and was smiling, her lovely blue eyes glistening, as she stood gathering the plates together.

'Can nothing be done for Penny? A cure?' asked Clare softly, when the girl had taken the pile of plates out to the back kitchen.

'Seems not. I forget the long words they used — some sort of paralysis, that it might only be temporary. But five years! We've given up hope. It was a tragic shock — ' Joseph arose abruptly, thrust back his chair and strode out, followed by the other two men.

'Those blasted Laytons!' At Clare's gasp of astonishment Timothy added, 'Aye, they're at the root of it all.' He sucked at his pipe a moment. 'But you stay, miss — we need the help.'

So Clare stayed on at the Cannings' farm and was soon as absorbed in the life there as though she had always belonged, and that Fate had led her there to find peace and happiness at last. The tormented years began to be wiped away, especially the time of fear and misery, the degradation of the final year or so.

The men, including the farm hands who stayed for the mid-day meal, licked their lips over her excellent cooking. They expected good square, nourishing meals and they got them. Martha chased through the housework and then went out to her beloved animals. Her face looked more relaxed as she milked their few cows and worked around the stables, dreaming of great improvements. Clare often watched her, stroking the soft nose of horse or cow as Martha worked. Turning away from watching her toss corn to the hens one day, Clare found the farmhand,

Louis, at her side. He had a habit of appearing behind her, his fine dark eyes frankly admiring her, and she never felt at ease in his company.

'So you are staying with us, Miss Bowers. That's fine.'

'Yes, I hope to stay for a long time.'

'It's much nicer with you here, and the food is good.'

'I'm glad you are satisfied.'

'Miss Martha can't cook.'

'It is easy when you enjoy it, and I've done a lot in my time. Now I must go. Penny seems to be looking for me.'

That was not exactly the truth, for Penny had started out for the moors carrying a basket. Clare had no intention of encouraging Louis. There was something about him she did not like. He was certainly a good-looking fellow with his trim moustache and sleeked-back dark hair, and he knew it, but Clare did not trust him. Given a chance he would take some shaking off. The other man, Dan, was a different proposition. He was an older, amiable man with rugged tanned features, a typical sturdy farmhand who went quietly and efficiently about his work.

'Can I come with you?' she asked Penny.

The girl nodded, eyes brightening, and held out her basket to show six brown eggs lying there, so that Clare would know that she was taking them to someone. The young black collie dog, Laddie, a white patch on his face and back, had come running back to welcome her and now ran circles round the two of them for a few minutes before setting off ahead over the crisp moorland turf. He was the youngest of the three dogs and was still playful and impulsive. The other two were working dogs. Sam was more subdued, fond of house and hearth. Shane looked on himself as Joseph's dog, following at his heels, obeying his commands. Where Joseph was, there Shane would be, too.

After a time Penny caught Clare's hand and turned aside into a narrow rutted lane towards a row of small stone cottages. Clare smiled at her, knowing that Penny was one of her chief reasons for staying in these parts. The girl seemed to have accepted her and seldom now had that scared, lost look, and as though she would run into hiding any minute.

Penny stopped by a small gate, opened it, then smiled and beckoned for Clare to follow her up the little path between trim beds of daffodils and bright aubrieta. She knocked once and at a soft reply within, lifted the latch and entered. A thin elderly woman sat in a corner chair, a pair of walking-sticks lying near at hand. Her face brightened at the sight of the young girl.

'Hello, Penny, my dear. Sit down a while.' The old eyes peered out of their wrinkled folds at Clare in the background. 'You've brought a friend with you?'

Penny nodded and drew Clare forward. Clare took the wrinkled hand. 'I'm staying at the farm,' she said.

'Helping them with some of the work.'

'Aye, I heard they were shorthanded. Help is hard to come by these days. I don't know what I'd do without Mrs. Pilling, and Terry can't do everything. Sit down, Miss — er — '

'Bowers. Clare Bowers.'

The grey head bowed. 'Nice name. Mrs. Pilling will be in soon. She'll get us a drink of tea. So these eggs are for me, Penny — bless you, dear.' As Penny went to put the eggs into a dish on the table, the elderly woman smiled at Clare. 'I'm glad Penny has found a friend at last. She's a lonely little girl, aren't you, dear?'

Looking a little disturbed at that, the girl went over to the small window and stared out. 'Terry should be along soon, Penny. My grandson,' the woman told Clare.

Suddenly the latch lifted again and a short, round, middle-aged woman came in. 'Oh, you've got visitors, Mrs. Grant,' she said, halting on the threshold.

'Come in, Mrs. Pilling, it's all right.

This is a friend of Penny's, Miss Bowers.'

'And I suppose you'd like me to get you all a cup o' tea.'

Mrs. Grant smiled, understanding the woman's crisp tone. 'Take no notice of her, Miss Bowers. She spoils me, you know.'

'She has arthritis bad,' said Mrs. Pilling, moving over towards the kitchen in the rear. 'Takes her ten minutes to cross the room these days.'

'I have to sleep downstairs, too, to my shame,' put in Mrs. Grant, waving a hand towards a narrow bed against a wall. 'But those steep stairs are beyond me.'

'And it took us some time to make you see sense about that,' came Mrs. Pilling's caustic remark from the back.

They were in a circle drinking the tea when there were footsteps on the flagged path outside and Mrs. Grant's grandson came in. A tall, broad young fellow in his early twenties, with a fresh complexion and curly fair hair.

'Hello, Gran. Company again? You lucky girl,' he said cheerfully. His eyes sought out Penny and he smiled. 'Hello, Penny.' He patted her head in passing and she smiled up at him confidently. Adoration shone from her deep blue eyes. Here was someone she trusted, thought Clare, someone of whom she was truly fond. Even as the thought passed through her mind, Penny took her hand and put it in Terry's.

'She wants us to be friends,' said Terry, gripping hard.

'Miss Bowers,' explained his grandmother. 'She's living up at Moorlands.'

'Call me Clare, please, all of you. I'm sure Penny thinks of me like that.' The young girl nodded in agreement, her face happier than Clare had ever before seen it.

'Come and see Cindy's puppies, Penny,' Terry said, draining his cup and putting it down. She was on her feet at once, eager to be off.

Mrs. Grant chuckled as the two young people went out. 'She's a deal brighter than she was a year ago, poor lass. I don't know how Terry managed to break the ice.'

They were away about ten minutes and when they returned Penny, her pretty face shining with happiness, was cuddling a honey-coloured retriever puppy in her arms. A golden satin-coated bitch followed close on their heels, anxious about her offspring.

'What a beautiful dog,' said Clare.

'Yes, and her five puppies will be almost like her, I think,' said Terry.

'I can see Penny will want to adopt one,' laughed Clare, as the puppy clambered up to the girl's neck and licked her chin.

'I don't suppose her dad will want another dog. They have three already,' he said, as Penny turned eagerly towards him.

'I don't think her dad will deny her anything,' said Clare.

'That's correct,' joined in Mrs. Grant. 'Joseph Canning has his faults but he's real good to Penny, and there's plenty of room for animals over at Moorlands.'

'Come on then, Penny,' said Terry. 'Come and put your mark on the one you like best.'

'I took it that they were all alike,' laughed Clare.

'Penny will find something different, don't you worry, if only a couple of hairs,' he chuckled.

'Good friends, aren't they?' said Clare, when Mrs. Pilling followed them out with the tea-tray, and she was alone with the old lady.

'Yes, he's made life happier for the poor girl, I'm sure, but I'm afraid — well, she depends on him too much.'

'She is so timid with most people.'

'That's right, so it's a relief to see how she's taken to you, because Terry is a young man — and young men are undependable. The girls are all making a fuss of him. I wouldn't want Penny to get hurt.'

'She is very young, too, so plenty of time for both of them,' said Clare, but she knew there was some sense in what Mrs. Grant said. Penny so lonely, nervous and wary of all strangers, having found someone she could like and trust, would tend to idolise and try to possess him.

They set off back over the moors at last, Penny skipping over the tough grasses and prickly gorse happily, no doubt dreaming of her new puppy. At one point they skirted a little copse of stunted thick trees and bushes where Clare had noticed bluebells growing. She was determined to get a bunch one day soon to brighten up the kitchen. Penny's gaiety lasted till they drew near some meadows bordering their farm, then she stopped abruptly, digging her heels into the ground. Surprised, Clare stared at her face. It had its strained, withdrawn look once more, wiped clear of that afternoon's happiness. She looked about her for enlightenment.

'What's the matter, Penny?' The girl shook her head and turned aside. 'Let's go this way, Penny, it's much nearer.'

Yet Penny shook her head again and made for a gate some way off. Astounded, Clare looked about her once more for a reason for that sudden change of mood. Nothing but cows and the narrow path taking a short cut through a meadow to the farm outbuildings. What had alarmed her? She fondled the animals in their stalls, but perhaps she was frightened when they were all loose, roaming at random. All the same that was hard to believe, pondered Clare, running after her. Then something must have reminded her of other things . . .

It was a pity the girl could not get away from here, thought Clare, feeling shut away from her again, if this place held such painful memories for her. A terrible tragedy, five years ago, Joseph had said, but nobody seemed prepared to talk about it. She did not want to annoy them by probing, either, because she had her own problems and did not want to leave here yet — the most peaceful haven she had known for a long time.

3

Joseph met Clare and Penny as they came round the house and into the cobbled yard. 'Where have you been? I wondered where you two had got to.' The stern lines of his face relaxed a little and he ruffled Penny's thick auburn hair. 'I don't like Penny to be too long away, and I hoped she would be with you, Clare.'

'We've been delivering some eggs,' replied Clare, with a quick glance at her young companion.

'Mrs. Grant, I suppose.'

'Yes, a sweet old lady.'

'You met her grandson, too, no doubt,' said Joseph dryly.

As Penny's colour deepened, Clare said, 'They have about five new puppies and Penny is going to have one.'

'My dear girl, haven't you enough with Shane, Sam and Laddie?' Then as his daughter gripped his arm with both her hands, deep blue eyes beseeching, Joseph said reluctantly, 'All right, all right, you little witch. But you look after him yourself, mind, and see he keeps off Layton's land.'

She nodded excitedly. If only she could speak and give real expression to her joy! sighed Clare.

'What with Penny and her dogs and cats and Martha with her horses!' exclaimed Joseph, raising his hands helplessly.

'Martha never seems so happy as when in the stables.'

'If you stay with us, Clare, she'll have the farm chockful of animals again.'

'Laytons had better look out, then.'

He gave her a strange look. 'Nothing would give me greater satisfaction than to see them sink under.'

His smile was gone, his customary sour expression back, and he went on his way. There was a cloud over Moorlands. That 'terrible tragedy' had changed Joseph, too — changed all of them. Joseph, ruddy-faced, russet hair, had probably been a jolly, good-natured fellow at one time.

'You been here a week or two,' said old Timothy to Clare that night, rocking his chair gently, 'and no post come for you yet.'

After a slight surprised pause, she said, 'There's no one to write. I have no one.'

'No one at all? That's bad — to be alone in the world.' Clare felt all the others' eyes on her, watching, speculating. 'Not even a cousin anywhere?'

'Not that I know of.'

'Then there's nothing to prevent you stopping here, is there? We ought to adopt her, Joseph.' There was a tense silence, then he added, 'Very odd for a girl to have no one. We don't even know where she comes from.'

Joseph's knife clattered against his plate. 'Does it matter, Father? Clare can stay as long as it suits her.'

'It's certainly been much pleasanter

for me since she took over,' said Martha hopefully.

Clare looked at the elderly man as he chuckled, and she was almost sure he winked at her before bending to knock his smelly old pipe against the grate. No doubt he would always be curious about her and ask questions, but she felt he wanted her to stay and in a devious way he was getting her firmly implanted in his family.

'I hope you'll stay a long time,' said Martha.

'For Penny's sake, at least,' murmured Joseph.

Clare looked across and met Penny's eloquent eyes, more persuasive than any words. 'I'll be pleased to stay, thank you. It's so nice to be — needed.' She had almost said 'wanted' but she felt that was an unfortunate word and shivered, remembering . . .

Next day, thinking of the vivid bluebells in the dell, Clare went over to gather some, with only Sam the thick-haired sheepdog for company. He had been lying in a sunny patch of the yard and, when she stooped to pat him, got up and followed her on her leisurely walk.

It was a good way down to the copse and beyond it the moors rose to quite a height, and she could see the rugged grey walls and chimneys of Hilltops, the Laytons' place. It was quiet and shadowy in the thick, bushy little wood. Sam lay down on the outskirts, waiting for her, as though he preferred the open moors. She trod carefully over the moist ground towards the thick wad of bluebells.

She had picked quite a tidy bunch when a stern voice demanded, 'What are you doing here?'

She had been so bent on her gathering that she had not heard him approach over the mossy ground. A tall, well-proportioned young man. Sunburnt, with short dark hair and a quiff with a bronze streak, and unsmiling blue eyes. She smiled uncertainly before his grim look. 'There are so many bluebells — I thought a few wouldn't be missed.'

'You're like all strangers, ruining the countryside.'

'I'm not pulling them up by the roots,' she said indignantly.

'You're trespassing. Where are you from?'

'Does it matter?' As he waited, eyeing her as though she were a wayward child, she said, 'I'm living at Moorlands, Cannings' farm.'

He gave a queer laugh. 'I might have known Cannings were at the back of it. Nobody else wanders here. So you are Joseph's new woman that I've heard about.'

'I am not Joseph's woman — nor anybody else's come to that!' Clare pulled herself up to her full height. 'I'm living — and working — there.'

'All right, if you say so.' He tapped his boots with the riding-crop he was holding. 'All the same you shouldn't be here. This is our land — it belongs to Hilltops. Even the dog knew better than

52

to come down here.' As she glanced back to where Sam waited on a rise of the ground beyond — 'Since he had some shot fired over his head one day.'

At this Clare froze with anger. 'I've been warned about you people at Hilltops and now I believe them. I think you're hateful. All this fuss over a bunch of wild flowers! Here, take them! I want nothing of yours!' She tossed the bluebells at his feet and hurried away.

His laugh followed her. 'You little idiot!' — but she ran up the hill with burning cheeks, Sam leaping after her. Joseph's new woman, indeed!

A few minutes later she slowed to a walk, thinking things over. Why had she lost her temper like that — just because he made her feel like a naughty six-year-old kid? Getting angry over a stupid bunch of flowers! She wondered what had caused the feud between the two farms, and who was the most to blame. Knowing the severe Cannings quite well by now, she guessed it was as much one as the other. As she entered the farmyard, Louis came over to her as he usually did, no doubt glad to talk to someone new.

'Why isn't there a notice or a fence by that small copse?' Clare asked him. 'How was I to know it was out of bounds? I only wanted to get some bluebells for the house.'

He grinned widely, showing straight firm teeth. 'You went in the copse?' He chuckled. 'Didn't you get your flowers?'

'I did, but I got caught red-handed. Naturally, I threw them back at him. If the man had behaved normally I would have apologised!'

'Man?'

'Tall, dark-haired young fellow.'

'It would be Richard Layton, then. Eh, the old master will be right pleased to hear you've taken a rise out of one of those fellows.'

He put out a hand to help her over the uneven worn step to the kitchen, but she shrank from his touch. There was a wicked gleam in his dark eyes, his smile sly, and she was still wary of people. The past few years had hardened her.

Of course Louis spread the news. Perhaps he hoped to annoy the Cannings, but old Timothy was amused. 'So you put that young scoundrel in his place, did you, Clare?' he laughed.

Her face burned, thinking of that afternoon. 'No one told me that part belonged to them. What does a handful of wild flowers matter, anyway? You'd think I was digging up his crops.' She felt now that she was making too much of such a paltry incident, but it was the principle of the thing. She glanced at Joseph. He had said nothing but he was scowling.

'Right glad you didn't bow down to him, any road,' said Timothy. 'You keep away from them, my girl. They'll never do you no good.'

Joseph scraped back his chair and went out to the yard, snatching his cap off the pegs as he went.

'Now, where's he off to?' grunted his father. 'Down to visit his woman, I reckon.'

'Well, if Dora Walters can help to make him more amiable all the better,' said Martha.

As the days passed, the rambling old white farmhouse, with its meadows and vegetable fields bounded by fresh green moors, was becoming a second home to Clare. Yet she was always on the watch, moving quickly out of sight if an unknown car approached the farm. She tried to hide her uneasiness if a stranger called yet felt that Timothy, who missed so little, must have noticed sometimes and wondered. They were busy weeding the onion bed one day when Penny came rushing towards them. She looked flushed and agitated, her hands waving in the air, imploring for help.

'Now, what's to do with our Penny?' grumbled the old man. 'Poor kid, she gets so worked up not being able to speak.'

'I'll go with her and see what's wrong,' said Clare. 'You sit down a while and rest, Mr. Timothy. I'll finish this when I come back.'

With his hand on his aching back he was glad of the chance to relax. He sank down on a creaking bench in the sunlight and took out his well-worn pipe. Taking Penny's hand she ran with her to the outlying lands. The girl stopped by a gate to a small meadow and showed Clare some lumps of sugar she held in her other hand. A few cows lazed in a nearby corner but there was no sign of the plump little horse.

'You mean you can't find Tilly, is that it?' As Penny nodded, Clare said, 'She won't be far, I expect. We'll see if she's up in the yard.'

Louis was by the stables, curry combing a sleek brown horse. 'Aye, Tilly was here,' he said. 'She followed us when I brought the others in. Have you lost your little pet, then, Penny girl?' he teased, catching at the girl's slender arm.

She pulled away, a spark of annoyance in her blue eyes. He laughed. 'Don't take on so, ducky. She'll have gone in her stable, I guess. You know

Tilly — does just as the mood takes her. A proper woman.'

But Tilly was not in her stable. 'She's gone off again?' Clare stared at Penny, remembering the mare ambling down the lane that day some time ago now. As Penny nodded, looking distressed — 'We'll soon find her. Come along.'

They walked down to the narrow road skirting the moors, between low ragged hedgerows, then with still no sign of Tilly they turned their attention to the moors themselves. Soft green turf and fresh gorse in yellow clumps, the open spaces no doubt tempting to a wanderer such as Tilly. Penny suddenly pointed. Clare saw the horse's round shape against the skyline, trotting determinedly on towards forbidden territory — the Laytons' farm.

'Wait here, Penny. Let me have that sugar,' said Clare. 'I'll get her to come back.'

She ran over the intervening sloping moorlands and through a gap in the hedge that Tilly had taken, into their neighbours' property. She called her name softly, gradually gaining on her. Tilly took notice of Clare at last and halted, turning and tossing her head, her warm brown eyes on the out-stretched hand with sugar.

'Come on, Tilly, sugar.' The horse nibbled at the one lump on Clare's palm, eyeing her dubiously. 'Come along home, Tilly. You are getting too fat for a lady to be rambling about like this.'

Tilly was persuaded by her soft caressing voice and they were walking back the way she had come, when another horse cantered up towards them and Richard Layton's cool voice said, 'So! You again! What is this attraction our lands have for you?'

Looking beyond him, Clare saw a string of fine-limbed horses returning to the stable-yard. Evidently they had been exercising the animals over the moors and someone had spotted the intruders.

'It's Tilly — the horse,' said Clare,

clutching at Tilly's thick mane. 'She wandered off and I was the only one available for tracking her down.'

He flicked a riding-crop against his boot as before. 'No respect for other people's property, have you?' he said.

'I'm sorry. I got her as soon as I could.'

'You want to chain that animal up. She's a crazy creature, no sense at all.'

Clare gave him a look of scorn then put another piece of sugar under Tilly's nose. 'Come on, Tilly, let's get away from this horrible place. It's no place for you.'

She could have sworn she heard him chuckle as she led the amiable little mare away. He made her feel so ruffled and small, aways finding her at a disadvantage, trespassing. Yet her face cleared as Penny saw them and ran to meet them. Her joyful face was worth all the disagreeableness.

'We'll have to keep her from roaming, Penny,' sighed Clare; 'but I don't know how we are going to do it.'

The mare was in no mood for escaping again, though. A few days later in the early hours, her foal was born. Martha had sat up with her and she came in at breakfast time, looking untidy and soiled, her bun of hair dropping to her neck, but her face triumphant.

'Tilly is marvellous,' she said. 'A beautiful foal — a perfect little fellow. Come and see, all of you.'

They all followed towards the stable where Tilly had spent the restless night, old Timothy shambling behind them with his stick. Joseph took one glance at the elegant little black foal with the white blaze on its forehead and white forelocks. 'My God!' he exclaimed.

Martha ran her hand down the slender long legs. 'See what she's given us. He has the makings of a perfect racehorse.'

'There's no horse here that's sired that gradely one,' said Louis.

Tilly licked her sprightly offspring with motherly pride. Timothy chuckled behind them. 'Just let Laytons get an eye on that one and there'll be murder.'

'That's the answer,' said Joseph gravely. 'I saw it at once. It's that handsome black of Laytons, same markings. Tilly's been over there — she was missing two days once.'

'I don't care,' said Martha happily. 'We've got a racehorse now — and it won't be the last. I'll make something of this horse or die in the attempt.'

'Sure is a beauty,' said Dan, with awe in his rough voice. 'What are you going to call him?'

Penny was fondling the new foal, her face wreathed in smiles, kissing its soft ears and nose, unable to speak but delight and admiration in her every movement.

'Penny's Pride,' murmured Clare, watching her.

'Of course,' said Martha. 'Penny's Pride. What better name could he have? We'll make a winner out of him yet, won't we, Penny?'

The young girl nodded excitedly, her arms about the foal's neck. Clare was deeply pleased for both of them. No one gave a thought to the Laytons, though Clare felt there was something due to them when their stallion had sired such a handsome creature.

'You'll be grumbling about my cooking if you don't come at once and eat up,' said Clare, pushing her way through the admiring group to the door.

'Nothing matters today but Tilly and the foal. My red-letter day!' Martha knelt by the new arrival with an expression full of worship. She was lost in a cloud of happiness. Meals, nothing else would matter to Martha this day.

'Looks like our luck's changed at long last,' muttered Joseph, following Clare back over the yard. 'It's come with you, Clare.'

He spoke warmly, unusually amiable, but she avoided his gaze. They all seemed to be depending on her too much. Though the morning was sunny she shivered. Ill-luck had dogged her footsteps before running away. If he knew more about her, perhaps he would not be so sure . . .

4

In the days following, Martha cossetted Tilly and spent most of her time with the new pony. Even when they were in the meadow she leant on the gate, watching lithe little legs skipping around the mother and from one end of the meadow to the other. Even though so young, tossing his dark head proudly, as though conscious of his fine breed.

Though Tilly was busy with her role of mothering and guarding her foal, it was a skittish dog that got Clare into trouble again. Of the three dogs at Moorlands, Laddie was the youngest and mischievous. He had taken to Clare from the start and she had hard work to get away from the farm without him. Walking on the moors, though, she was glad of his company, but the day came when he espied a rabbit and was off like a shot, round in circles and then down a dip in the moors. Careering towards the Laytons' lands, bent on catching that little thing with the bobbing white tail.

'Oh, no!' groaned Clare. He ignored all Clare's commands to return and she went in hot pursuit. The Laytons might shoot on sight. They wouldn't want a dog scouting around their property. As he disappeared beneath a bush she dived after him, clutching at his waving tail, and they both went down together tangled up in thorns and branches, down into a deep ditch. She cried with pain as thorns prodded her skin, trying to fight a way out, and presently a stout stick swept the undergrowth away and strong hands dragged her out.

'You certainly make a habit of trespassing over here,' said a well-known cool voice.

'Not from choice,' she retorted, plucking thorns from her hands. 'It was the dog's fault. He was only after a rabbit, but I didn't want you shooting him when he was doing no harm.'

'What would you think if our animals roamed all over your land?'

'It's not my fault if the Canning animals haven't learnt to behave.'

'It no doubt suits the Cannings to annoy us, to have our corn trampled, our fences broken — '

'Don't exaggerate, Mr. Layton. What harm has been done?'

Bristling with anger, she forced herself to meet the bright blue eyes beneath the thatch of dark, bronze-streaked hair, and to her surprise saw the flicker of a smile soften the stern mouth.

'I think the most harm has been done to yourself. Here,' he said, taking a white handkerchief from his top pocket, 'wipe your face. It's bleeding. You've scratched it.'

'I am all right, thank you.' She took a handkerchief from her own pocket and mopped at her face. At a snort from his restless horse, pawing the ground behind him, she paused, staring at the handsome stallion. Silky black coat, white blaze between flashing eyes, proud erect head and white forelocks ... here, without a doubt, was the father of Penny's Pride.

'Don't worry about Rocket,' said Layton, jerking at the reins. 'He is only anxious to move on.'

'I was just admiring him,' said Clare, forgetting past differences. 'He's beautiful.'

'And he knows it. He's a handful. Nothing he likes better than the open moors.'

'Does he roam?'

'He's broken away once or twice, more's the pity. He's a fine racer but somewhat unpredictable. He's done well for us but one never knows with him — he could turn round and chase the opposite way.'

Clare felt the urge to laugh. She wondered how long it would be before they saw Tilly's foal and perhaps guess the truth.

'What's the matter here?' suddenly

asked a deep voice, as another rider came up alongside Rocket.

'Nothing really, sir,' said Clare, then stopped abruptly, staring up at the newcomer. 'Oh, sorry — ' At first she had thought it was another man of the Layton family, with the dark hair clipped close to the head like a shining black cap, the jodhpurs and plain white shirt top. But this person — though so masculine, with features grave like the other's and riding like a man — this was a woman.

'My sister Jess,' said Richard Layton. 'Miss — er — '

'Bowers. Clare Bowers.'

'And what Jess doesn't know about horses is nobody's business,' went on Richard firmly. 'We'd get nowhere without her.'

'Has there been an accident?' asked Jess, looking curiously at Clare's dishevelled face and hair. 'There's blood on her face.'

'I fell through the hedge. I always seem to be in the wars,' said Clare.

'That seems a peculiar thing to do.' Jess stared at the gap in the hedge.

'It was the dog's fault — Cannings' dog,' explained Richard. 'You'd better be taking him away, Miss Bowers. He's making Rocket uneasy.'

'I hope I can keep out of your way in future,' said Clare. 'Come along — you stupid dog!'

Naturally they noticed her scratched face at tea-time. 'My goodness,' said Joseph. 'What have you been doing to yourself?'

'I slipped and fell through a hedge.'

Timothy chortled. 'Can tell you're no country girl. What were you doing?'

Clare told a half-truth. 'Laddie was after a rabbit and got stuck in the hedge. I was trying to get him out.'

'If you go on like this, tearing your face to pieces, we'll have to keep you indoors,' said Joseph.

'I must be getting clumsy, and I'd better be off to that oven,' said Clare, rising hastily, 'or there'll be another accident.'

The big fruit cake was not quite ready, but when she took it from the oven fifteen minutes later, Timothy was behind her, breathing in the tempting smell. 'My! that's a beauty,' he admired. 'I'll never stomach Martha's cooking again after this — '

'It's not to be eaten for a while yet,' she said firmly. 'It's for Penny's birthday — but there's some sausage rolls for your supper. Go on, sample one,' she laughed, as his fingers hovered longingly over the tray of rolls she had baked earlier.

'I'd like to take Penny somewhere for her birthday,' said Clare that evening. 'I wonder what she would like?' She glanced at the girl who had looked up suddenly with startled blue eyes. 'She never gets away from here for a change.'

'There's nothing in Lambreck,' said Joseph.

'Sometimes the church gets up a bazaar or a little dance, but there's nothing just now,' said Martha.

'There's a cinema at Randgate,

though, isn't there?' suggested Clare. 'We'd be there in the car in no time.'

Randgate, their nearest town eight miles away, was not large, but its shops were good and there was more activity.

'There's a circus coming there — the week of Penny's birthday,' said Timothy. 'She likes animals.'

Clare wondered how he knew all the news. The old man spent half his life in his rocking-chair, yet he seemed to know all that was going on. His quick eyes and ears picked up everything.

'Would you like that, Penny?' she asked.

Penny was still staring, hesitating, then she slowly nodded.

'I think she will go with you,' said Martha; 'but she wouldn't go with anyone else, except Joe or me.'

They often talked about Penny, over and around her, as though they imagined she was deaf as well as dumb, and Clare felt it was a mistake. It must be embarrassing for the girl, besides treating her as a child, forgetting her seventeenth birthday was looming up. Clare changed the subject. She would ask Penny again in private nearer her birthday.

Clare walked into Richard Layton next time in the post office. It was going to prove impossible to avoid the people from Hilltops, unless one kept within their own gates like Timothy. Or walk past them, ignoring them, which Clare felt she would be incapable of doing. She nodded and murmured a polite 'good afternoon' and went over to a small counter, turning over the few odd magazines. He finished at the postal counter and went out, but when she left the shop he was still there, waiting for her.

'Can I give you a lift home, Miss — er — Bowers?'

'I have my own car, thank you.' She turned to walk away, but he followed, putting out a hand to detain her.

'Why are you scared of me?'

'I am not scared of you,' she said coolly.

'I'm sorry I made such a fuss about the horse and the dog, but I hate to see destruction — and just that alone can't explain your attitude. What have the Cannings been saying?'

She met his steady blue eyes, such a contrast to his crisp black hair. 'I know they dislike you for some reason and that's all.'

'I have done them no harm, neither has the rest of my present family.' She wanted to move on but his serious face compelled her to stay. 'There was trouble five years ago and in the past, but they can't blame any of us for it. They grudge us our success.'

'It's nothing to do with me, Mr. Layton.'

'You've been warned off, though, is that it?'

'Yes. Now, if you don't mind, I must be on my way.'

'All right, Miss Bowers, if that is how you want it.'

That was *not* how she wanted it, but what could she do about it? In spite of their bad beginning, she liked his strong, earnest face, his wavy dark hair and intense blue eyes, and she would have liked to be friendly with him if it were not for the Cannings. She paused and looked back as someone else came along, passing the time of day with Richard Layton in a warm, pleasant voice. She watched the woman walk to the end of the narrow street — a tall, well-made woman of middle-age, with hair still dark and smoothed to the head.

'That is Dora Walters,' said Richard, studying her interested face. 'I take it you haven't met yet. She's a close — friend — of Joseph Canning's.'

She felt herself flush at his slight hesitation before and after 'friend'. 'Joseph's woman' he would have liked to say. 'I expect we shall meet sometime. Now I really must be off. I've been away long enough and there's plenty to do.'

He watched her with a strange expression as she got into her car and drove off, without a backward glance, having apparently forgotten him already. Clare had indeed forgotten him. Her mind was on Dora Walters, the smiling-faced woman who had just passed. No wonder Joseph was attracted by her, but would he marry her? He seemed satisfied with things as they were, especially since Clare helped so much and Martha was working all day long to build up the farm again. He and Dora Walters would be an ideal match for each other, though, she thought, as she slowed down past the potato field, seeing his big body and reddish hair bent over the work there. Why had his wife been so delicate, dying so young? Clare wondered what she had been like. There didn't seem to be a photograph of anyone in the whole place.

Timothy was sitting in his rocking-chair, puffing his pipe and swaying gently as he pored over a newspaper that was about a week old, that someone must have passed on to him. Now and again he glanced up, watching her as she moved about, getting their meal ready.

'What do you think of Lambreck?' he asked once.

'It's how I like it — just a quiet little country village. I hope the new estate on the hill won't creep in and spoil it.'

'Reckon most of 'em go over to Randgate for shopping, and there's vans calling round up there, too.'

After a moment, Clare said, 'I saw Miss Dora Walters today.'

'Mrs., my girl — she's a widow woman. Comely wench, isn't she?'

'I thought she looked very nice.'

'But I bet she can't cook as good as you.' As Clare was silent, he went on, 'You're a right gradely lass, Clare' — and that was a rare compliment coming from old Timothy.

A day or so later Clare iced Penny's cake in white and pink. The girl watched and helped a little, her cheeks glowing with pleasure as the sugar flowers and twirls took shape.

'It's nearly your birthday, Penny. We'll go to the Circus, shall we?'

Penny nodded and clapped her hands, eyes sparkling. Clare guessed it had been in the girl's mind since it was first mentioned and by now she was really eager to go. She had been puzzled what to give her for a birthday gift, and decided on a new silk scarf she had never used. It was flame-coloured with little green leaves embroidered in one corner, and was still wrapped in tissue-paper . . . but she almost ruined the day. Penny backed away, her hands trembling, her expressive eyes showing alarm.

'Oh, I'm sorry,' said Clare hastily, withdrawing the scarf and turning to Joseph. 'Does it upset Penny to receive presents?'

'It's the colour,' said Martha quietly. 'It brings back memories — bad memories.'

Joseph left the breakfast table and strode to the door. 'Her mother wore a scarf like that,' he said.

'I'm so sorry, Joseph. I'd no idea, or else I would never — '

'It's all right. You were not to know. It was just unfortunate.'

The door closed behind Joseph. 'If only someone would tell me more about Penny's mother and what happened to rob Penny of her voice,' said Clare miserably, seeing the girl had vanished, too. 'Then I wouldn't make these dreadful mistakes.'

'We don't care to speak of it. We try to forget,' said Martha.

'We all have our troubles, our bad times,' said Clare, her hands clasped over a chair-back, thinking of her own sufferings. 'I was terribly lonely and unhappy till I came here. If I could help Penny in any way — '

'Let sleeping-dogs lie, so they say,' put in Timothy, pressing tobacco down in his pipe. 'The wickedness is buried in the grave with Penny's mother — let the woman now lie in peace.'

In some way Penny's tragedy was

linked up with her mother's death, thought Clare. Something awful had happened here — five years ago — but it didn't seem as though she would ever know what. She went in search of Penny and put her arms about her.

'Forget it, Penny dear. I'll buy you something else. We'll leave early and look at the shops first.'

For a moment Penny's face, wet with tears, was pressed against her then, as Clare went on talking of the Circus and brighter things, she looked up at last and smiled.

That day, in spite of the poor start, turned out to be a thoroughly happy day for Penny. Watching her interested, glowing face, Clare suspected that every birthday for years had been just as ordinary and humdrum as any other day. It seemed like treating her as a child again taking her to a circus, but it was her choice, doting on animals as she did. After the show they went around to the quarters in the rear to have a close look at the clever animals they had admired. The floor was thickly strewn with sawdust and the enclosure was warm and rather overpowering with the animal smells. Reluctant to leave, Penny went back to the elephants, leaving Clare stroking the shining head of a cream-coloured horse.

'Good afternoon, Miss Bowers,' said a woman's contralto voice behind her. 'Quite beautiful, aren't they?'

Clare turned to Jess Layton. She stood, legs astride, dressed as usual in masculine style, plain shirt, no fripperies. 'Yes, they are. I'd love to own one.'

'Yes, quite beautiful,' said Jess again, 'and I'm always on the look-out for faults. It was a good show, too. I suppose you've been?'

'Yes. I brought Penny — it's her birthday today.'

'Oh, is it? I'll move on in a minute, then. I don't want to embarrass the poor kid.'

'She's gone back to the elephants, I think.'

'It's all so stupid. No reason in these

days not to be friendly, though I suppose Joseph Canning has cause enough to be eternally bitter. I was hoping to see more of you, Miss Bowers.'

'I wish you and Martha could get together,' said Clare impulsively. 'She is mad on horses — you could be such a help to her. She has dreams of rearing race-horses . . . '

'Has she, indeed?' Jess smiled wryly. 'Good luck to her. If I can ever be of any help, of course . . . ' She moved away then looked back. 'Come over to Hilltops some day, Miss Bowers. You'd be welcome.'

'I ought to offer you a lift home — ' Clare hesitated.

'Don't worry, my dear girl,' said Jess. 'I have my own reliable transport. Archer waits for me over at the Inn.' At the other's blank look, she added, 'My favourite steed, Archer.'

Clare watched her walk away with her swinging stride, thinking that wherever Jess Layton was there would be a horse not far away. Her life was horses from morn to night, and often through the night as well, no doubt.

Penny was coming back and Terry Grant was with her. He was laughing and holding her hand. 'Look what I found tangled up with the elephants,' he said.

Penny was prettily flushed, looking happy, smiling.

'Do you know that it is Penny's birthday?' said Clare.

Quickly the girl held up a hand and showed the silver charm bracelet on her slender wrist.

'So he did know. Terry gave you that, Penny?'

'I've been carrying it about hoping to see her,' he said.

Clare turned to the young man. 'Is it possible — how about coming up to tea with us, Terry?' Penny tugged at his arm, her lips trying to form words.

'I'd like to come very much, if you think I'll be welcome.'

'We'll give it a try, anyway. If you've

both finished here we'll go for the car.'

Martha met them as they walked into the yard at Moorlands. 'Hello, Terry,' she said. 'How is your grandma?'

'About the same, Miss Martha. She does her best.'

'I've asked Terry to stay to tea,' said Clare. 'I thought it would be nice for Penny's birthday.'

Martha paused, her face expressionless. 'All right.' A ghost of a smile crossed her lips. 'I'm sorry — I was taken by surprise. We're not used to visitors.'

'If you're sure it's all right — '

'Of course. Why shouldn't it be? We've known Terry long enough. And I suppose he gave you that?' Martha added, as Penny displayed her new bracelet. 'He spoils you.'

Clare had prepared a few delicacies for tea besides the prettily decorated cake, and the meal passed over pleasantly enough. Penny looked so delighted with everything, with Terry waiting on her and chatting about this and that, so that only a hard heart could have denied her any of it. Timothy and Joseph were quiet and, except for a curt nod and look of astonishment at first, Penny's father had taken the unusual company in his stride, but Clare felt that he was annoyed. She knew for certain after Penny had gone to the gates with Terry to see him set off for home, when Joseph came up to the table she was clearing and stood looking down at her.

'I'd rather you didn't encourage Terry Grant to come here, Clare.'

She glanced up to meet his stern gaze, her face slightly flushed. 'I'm sorry, Joseph. I was only thinking of Penny and her birthday, and she knows Terry so well.'

'You ought to have asked me first.'

'It was on the spur of the moment, but I'd no right — taking so much on myself. I'm sorry. It won't happen again.'

'I don't want to dominate your life, Clare, but when it concerns Penny — '

'I don't think you need worry, Joseph. He seems a sensible, very nice young man.'

'I don't want Penny to get too attached to him — or to any fellow. It's difficult enough as it is. She's not a normal child — '

'Oh, please, Joseph, she is as normal as any of us except for the loss of her voice, and she is no longer a child. She is seventeen today and will have to gain confidence and make a life for herself. There is no reason why she shouldn't have a good life, marry some day a man who is sympathetic and understands — as I'm sure Terry does . . . ' Clare halted, aghast at herself, at letting words run away with her.

'It's good of you to do so much for Penny, Clare, and you've brought happiness into her life, but let it stop at that. I don't want her to grow too fond of Terry. She is too young.'

'Very well, Joseph. I'd no right to say so much. If Terry comes here again it won't be at my invitation.'

Clare went away and up to her room. From a window on the landing she had a fine view of the moors, burnished with the setting sun, and she could see two figures walking hand-in-hand. She smiled wryly. Joseph was too late with his demands. Clare suspected that Terry and Penny were already more than half in love with each other.

5

Clare often walked over the moors and stared over at Hilltops. It seemed such a pity they couldn't all be friends. Though glad of her present home, life was empty for her without friends outside their own close circle.

She often saw Jess Layton in the distance, exercising her horses and putting them through their paces, and she often saw her or Richard in the village — and managed to avoid them beyond a polite exchange of words.

Clare did most of the shopping for the Cannings with her little car, till one day in Randgate it started to behave oddly on the hill into the town. She parked it, found a garage and asked for it to be towed in and overhauled. Possibly the collision with the hedge had done more harm than they thought. She was stranded with her bags of groceries, waiting for the hourly bus when Richard Layton drove by. He took a wide sweep and came back to her.

'Surely not waiting for the bus, are you, Miss Bowers?'

'Yes, I am. My car has broken down.'

'Well, jump in. I'll run you home, that is if you don't mind going out of the way ten miles. I've a bit of business to see to first.'

'I'll be all right here, but thank you very much.'

He leant forward. 'Why are you still avoiding me?'

'I'm not. Well — we don't often see each other. I'm kept busy.'

'Why does it matter what the Cannings think? You are free to do as you like, aren't you?'

She hesitated, his searching blue eyes on her face, the quiff of hair fallen boyishly across his brow. She had been feeling so depressed and lonely that day. The Cannings were so uncommunicative, and it was a strain sometimes talking all the while to Penny with no real response. Why shouldn't she have some fresh company? 'All right, then,' she decided. 'I'd be glad of the lift.'

'That's fine.' He took her shopping-bags and put them over in the back while she went round and slid into the seat beside him.

As the car moved forward he said, 'You haven't answered my question. Why do you let the Cannings rule your life? You are free to come and go as you wish, aren't you? Not tied to them in any way? A relative or anything?'

'So many questions.' She stared at the dusty road ahead of them as they left Randgate for the open moors. 'I am no relative — no ties. I can do as I like — leave when I want.'

'Then let us be friends — Clare,' he said softly. 'I like you. Don't let the Cannings stand between us.'

She looked up, met his eager look and smiled. 'I'd like to be friends, Richard.'

'That's fine,' he said again. 'Now we

can make a fresh start.'

'They have been kind to me at Moorlands — when I was in a low state, so I don't want to upset them, naturally. That is the chief reason why — '

'Joseph Canning kind!' he said scornfully. 'Only for his own ends. He knows what a gem he has in you.'

Clare's colour rose, but she skipped over the last remark. 'I feel I must stay for Penny's sake. She seems to need me.'

'Poor kid.' He sighed and for some time after that was silent as the car raced on. She wondered how much he knew about the girl's tragedy, if anything, and if some day he would enlighten her.

Drawing into a quiet street of another small town she waited fifteen minutes while he kept his business appointment. When he returned he dropped a bunch of violets into her lap.

'With apologies for my ill-humour at our first meeting,' he said, climbing into the car. 'Straight from a patch in a friend's garden.'

'They're lovely.' She held the sweet-smelling flowers to her nose. 'I'm afraid I haven't been very lady-like, either — but can you blame me when I'm always having the Laytons' misdeeds rammed down my throat?'

At a high point on the moors he drew the car into the roadside and they sat a few minutes breathing in the fresh, tawny air that was blowing over the miles of open, deserted lands. Deserted except for thickly-coated, wild-looking sheep and a strange bird or two. The narrow road stretched and wound like a grey ribbon beyond them. Buttercups, harebells and meadowsweet mingled in the dry rustling grasses. Further away bracken made deep green patches, and in the far distance cultivated, walled fields with their various shades of green and yellow looked like a patchwork quilt.

'It's beautiful,' she breathed. She had never been to these parts before, did not even know such wild, colourful scenery still existed.

'I've enjoyed this afternoon, Clare,' he said, his eyes watching fleecy clouds drift across the pale-blue sky. 'We must do this again sometime.' As she was silent, he urged, 'Wouldn't you like to?'

'Yes, I would, but it's difficult for me, you know.'

'Don't let them keep you a prisoner.' As she gave a little shocked gasp, he bent nearer. 'We can meet somewhere to avoid gossip.'

'I suppose so.' After a moment she said, 'They say you steal their lands. So much of yours belonged to the Cannings once.'

'That's foolish talk. They've had bad luck and Joseph has been a poor manager, letting things drift once they started to go down. They needed money — offered land for sale, and we've bought it. They had a fair price. That's not stealing now, is it? It's jealousy — nothing but jealousy piled up on all the old frictions.'

She turned to him. 'What started all this? What happened five years ago? What has made all the Cannings hate you so? You must know. Tell me so that I can understand.'

'I was only eighteen, wrapped up in my own interests. It was all hushed up. About that time there was a big fire over there . . . They must tell you themselves, Clare.'

'I might as well try to open a locked safe. They'll never speak.'

Fire! thought Clare. Those crumpled-up blackened ruins of a building on the fringe of the farm that Joseph hated? Was it connected with Penny's disability — with the tragedy that haunted them all? Was that why any fire worried Penny? She had fled out of sight when Dan threw paraffin on a pile of garden rubbish and flames shot up.

'If only I could undersand why they hate you Laytons so much.'

'It's gone on for years, Clare. Fighting at school, nagging over property and animals. They even blamed us for the foot-and-mouth disease, which was nonsense. It's a wonder they don't blame us for the last bad winter. It all started with my great-great-grandfather, I think, who eloped with a cherished child daughter of the Cannings. Ever since then — any trouble it seems must come from us, and of course they hate to see their lands swallowed up by us.'

'And now I'd better be getting back before there's more trouble. I've no right to talk about them, really. It isn't my business, and the Cannings never probe into my private life.'

He laughed. 'I bet old Timothy does. There's nothing much he doesn't know about the villagers.'

'He's not a bad old soul.' She smiled. 'I can manage him.'

'I've wondered about you, too. What made you choose such an out-of-the-world spot?'

'I'm a lonely person.' Clare laughed nervously, staring at the ribbon of road, avoiding his clear gaze. 'I was on my way to Scotland, hoping to find a cottage or something, then I suppose — well, I got held up and took a fancy to these parts. These moors give one such a feeling of air and space — an away-from-it-all feeling.'

'I know what you mean. I could never stand town or city life, either.'

As the car slid forward, she told him, 'If it hadn't been for Tilly the horse, I'd have passed by, no doubt. She suddenly blocked the road and I dived into the ditch with the car.'

He laughed again. 'That crazy horse!'

Not so crazy as you think, thought Clare, stealing a glance at his attractive bronzed face, and thinking of the beautiful little foal Tilly had produced.

'There's an agricultural show on the outskirts of Randgate next Wednesday. Why don't you come? We shall be showing and also putting one or two horses in the afternoon races. Jess wants to put Black Satin through his paces, ready for bigger things.'

'Martha ought to go, at least. She is getting into her stride again — wants to build up the stock, especially horses.'

'I'll look out for you,' he said, undeterred.

'Drop me down here, please,' Clare said, as they came to a dividing of the roads. 'I'll go back over the meadows.'

'I can take you to the next bend.'

'No, Joseph might be in the fields.'

'Does it matter? Don't let him dictate to you, Clare.' She moved to open the door and he stopped the car.

'I'll be seeing you.'

'Don't depend on it. It might be wiser for me to snub you.' She smiled at him, yet annoyed with herself for liking him.

'Till next time, Clare. Take no notice of the Cannings.' He waved a hand airily and drove off.

To Clare's great surprise, Martha was eager to go to the agricultural show as soon as it was mentioned. 'We'll both go. Let the men manage their own meals for once. If there's anything I fancy — such as a horse . . . I've been saving a nest-egg for this opportunity.

We'll get a bargain there if anywhere.'

'I'll have my car back by then,' said Clare, delighted at her enthusiasm.

They left a meal prepared for the men and were just starting off on Wednesday when Louis ran up to them. 'Will you give me a lift, Miss Clare?' he said. 'Mr. Joseph says I can go and put my bit on the races.'

'All right, jump in.'

Penny in the back seat looked at him nervously as he dropped down beside her. Clare, seeing her shrink up against the corner, felt sorry for her, but what could she have done? The man was in order asking for a lift with the consent of Joseph Canning. They would be able to drop him when once at the Show. As Clare stopped the car in the wide grassy car park, Louis was the first to get out. He turned and, as Penny got up, lifted her out, holding her closely for a moment before putting her to the ground. Glancing at the girl's face, Clare saw that she was flushed and near to tears.

'Leave Penny alone, Louis,' Clare said. 'She's nervous of being touched.'

'All the more reason why I should look after her,' said Louis. 'She wouldn't be like that with Terry Grant.'

'She's used to him — he understands and is gentle with her. She trusts him.' Clare searched for words as Penny went ahead of them.

'She should be used to me by now. She's a comely lass and you can't expect a fellow not to notice. She'll have to learn, and we haven't enough girls about here to go round.'

'She isn't quite like other girls, so go easy with her.'

Clare disliked him for his stubbornness and cocksureness, and breathed a sigh of relief when presently he wandered off and they were on their own. Penny gave a wavering smile and came back to them. Martha had not taken much notice. Her eyes were already on the animals in the pens and the farmers starting to bargain. When they came to the horses parading they lost sight of her for a time, and Clare wandered about with Penny, the girl fondling the animals and they watched while some of the judging took place on the side.

'I've found what I want,' said Martha, joining them later in the day. 'Come and look.'

There were plenty of cattle and sheep for sale, and a few horses, and Martha led them up to a tall chestnut stallion.

'I wish I could be sure,' she said. 'I can afford him and I feel I could get some good racers out of him. I'd put him with Betsy.'

Clare looked at the quietly waiting horse, impressed. He had a certain air, undisturbed by the rabble around him, and his dark eyes were steady, watchful. Seeing Martha's interest the owner came over, stroked the horse, pushed back the lips to expose strong clean teeth, extolled over the well-arched neck and other fine points.

'It's a gamble, I suppose,' mused Martha.

It was then that Clare saw a familiar, masculine-attired figure approaching them. 'Here's Jess Layton,' she said, 'She'll advise you, Martha. What she doesn't know about horses — '

'If she knows I want him — ' faltered Martha, stiffening.

'Don't be silly, Martha. She's a good sort, and you can't afford to make mistakes.' Clare called Jess over to them. 'Hello, Jess. You know Martha, don't you? We'd like your advice.'

'Of course, if I can help.' Jess looked at Martha's glowering face doubtfully.

'Come on, Martha — ' urged Clare, smiling at them both, willing them to be friends.

Martha squared her shoulders. 'I'd like your opinion of this horse. You see — I want to improve the stock.'

'Oh, Red Dandy, yes.' Jess passed a hand over the horse's fine head and back. 'Some might say he has had his day, but to my mind he's a bargain. He's sired several good winners, and there's plenty of pride and confidence there yet, I'd say.'

'You think I'd do well to buy him, then?' Martha's eyes glittered.

'I do, indeed. It would be money well spent, I'm sure.' Jess looked at the other frankly. 'I'd like to see your farm on its feet again, Martha.'

'You two ought to get together sometimes,' said Clare, as Martha looked away, confused. 'Jess could help you such a lot, Martha.'

'Yes, it's time we disregarded the menfolk and were friends,' said Jess. 'Come over to Hilltops whenever you like. I'd be pleased to help — any time.' As Martha made no response, all her attention now on the horse, she shrugged. 'I'll be seeing you later, Clare. It's nearly time for the races, I think.'

Penny, who had listened to them with a rather startled, bewildered expression, now realised that her aunt was about to buy the beautiful stallion, and her face was alight with happiness as she stroked Red Dandy. They all enjoyed the racing soon afterwards. It was a bright fine day and the turf flew up from beneath speeding hoofs. Black Satin came in second.

'But he did well,' said Jess, as Clare watched her throw a blanket over the quivering black body. 'He's a strain of Rocket's, and he's shaping up well. He's going to be a first before long.'

'Just wait till I bring Penny's Pride along here,' breathed Martha. 'Can't you just imagine him having his first try-out here?'

'That will be the day, won't it, Penny?' said Clare affectionately. The girl nodded excitedly. They all knew they could expect great things from the elegant little foal.

'Did you have a bit on Black Satin?' a voice murmured in Clare's ear, as Penny edged away, having seen Terry over by the rails.

Clare swung around to Richard Layton. 'No, I don't bet.'

'I do and I won something. So come and have some refreshments with me.

Never mind about the Canning sister. You and Penny come.'

'I've been trying to make Jess and Martha be friends with each other.'

'Good lord! You've got more pluck than I have. How did it go?'

'A bit edgy, of course. I think Martha only tried to be polite because of me. They still tend to regard me as a guest in their house.'

'Well, maybe it's a start. It's something nobody else has tried to do.'

When the time came at last to leave for home, to Clare's relief there was no sign of Louis and she had no intentions of waiting for him. He could find his own way back. Knowing him, she knew he was never at a loss — he would cadge a lift from someone.

Next morning, finding herself alone with Martha, Clare made up her mind to get a few things straightened out.

'Martha, are you going to be friends with Jess Layton and call to see her?'

'No,' said Martha bluntly.

'Why not? She could be an enormous

help to you. Her life is horses — you've only to look at her to see that. You might even come to some arrangement over breeding — I mean, well, look at Tilly's foal . . . '

'Clare, how can I? Joseph would go tearing mad. We can't wipe out — things — just like that.'

'The men talk as though land has been stolen from them, but you know they were on the rocks and it was put up for sale. Who better to take it over than the adjoining farm? It's simply pure jealousy, Martha, and nothing else. If you were friends the land might even be shared in some way.'

Martha twisted the dish-cloth and stood staring at the water gurgling down the sink, her hands clasped tight on the edge. 'It isn't only that. There's a lot more to it than that.'

'Then tell me, Martha. It's time I knew what happened between these two farms. It won't go any further, I promise you.' As the other was silent, turning away, Clare persisted, 'Just because your great-grandfathers and aunts — or someone — wronged the family, it doesn't mean you have to go on hating the family — the young ones.'

Martha turned to her quickly. Her face was pale and set. 'We had a terrible time, Clare. Only five years ago. It turned Joe into a hard, bitter man — and poor little Penny . . . nothing has been the same since. Joe will never forget and forgive. If I go over there I think — I think he'd almost kill me.'

Chance remarks were slotting into place in Clare's mind, small, intangible things. Five years — a fire — Penny's fear of fire and her reaction to the bright scarf — and somewhere Laytons were mixed up with it all.

'I want to understand for Penny's sake, at least. Why was she so upset when I offered her the scarf for her birthday? Was it only because her mother had a similar one?'

'The scarf? Oh, yes.' Martha wiped a hand across her brow. 'Her mother wore one like that — '

'She saw her mother go out wearing that scarf. Come on, tell me, Martha . . . '

'It was evening. Penny was standing at her bedroom window brushing her hair and saw Ellen — her mother — go towards the big barn and hayloft at the end. Ellen often went there — there were apples and other things stored there, and soon afterwards — that evening — a man went inside after her. Penny would think nothing of that, of course, she had often seen him around. A cousin of the Laytons — he lived at Hilltops.' Martha sighed, then went on, 'Ellen was unfaithful to Joseph. How long it had gone on no one knows, but I think Joe was beginning to suspect. That night there was a terrible blaze, an oil-lamp overturned they think, and there was all that dry hay. Penny came tearing downstairs, screaming that her mother was in there. They got them out somehow, Ellen and the man — both — dead and soon after the barn collapsed, gutted. That night Penny lost her voice — and Joe turned to stone.'

'My God!' breathed Clare, after a stunned silence. 'I feel now perhaps I shouldn't have pressed you to tell me, Martha.'

'It's better you hear it from me than anyone else. Not that people talk about it. It seems to be a closed subject. In such a small place where everyone is known, they were all horrified. It was like a smear on the village. I don't think anyone ever mentions it now.' Martha picked up a brush and started to scrub the long table.

'Yet you still hate the family. A cousin, you say. You can't blame the rest of them for what happened. After all, it was their tragedy as much as yours. Ellen was as much at fault as their cousin.'

'You won't make Joe see it that way. There's always been hatred and wrong-doing with the two families, and he's afraid for Penny's sake. He guards her like a treasure. So you see, Clare, it's out of the question for me — to go anywhere near.'

After a moment's uneasy silence, Martha went on, 'I was glad when Joe took an interest in Dora Walters, she's been a good companion for him. And he's been a lot better since you came, Clare. So you see, even without knowing all this, you have helped us.'

'I wish I could do more. It's worse than I thought, and I feel dreadful now making you talk about it, Martha.'

'They say talk is better than bottling things up sometimes.' Martha sighed again. 'I think Joe might have married the Walters woman, but he seems to have no trust in women any more.'

And Clare, remembering his hard eyes, tight lips and unfriendly silences, felt she could not blame him.

6

That afternoon Clare, still feeling depressed and burdened with the Cannings' story, went for a stroll by herself. All the dogs were in the fields with the men, and Penny was somewhere playing with the new puppy that Terry had given her. Clare came to the blackened rubble of the old big barn and stood a moment gazing at it, picturing that night of terror. The leaping flames and Penny shrieking till at last, torn with shock, all sound left her throat — and Joseph with his heart turning to stone . . . But they all had each other while she, Clare, who had been through drastic trouble and suffering herself, had no one.

Why didn't Joseph rake over all the old ground and build another barn — anything — to hide those horrible scars that kept reminding them. He said nothing worthwhile would grow there — but had he ever tried? No wonder Penny shrank away from this corner. Clare strode quickly on. She glanced towards Hilltops against her will, wishing she could call and see Jess and Richard, then went walking on determinedly.

She had not gone so far when there was the beat of horse-hoofs behind her. She stopped and looked back, waiting, not at all surprised to see it was Richard. He was riding the big black, spirited horse and leading another quieter brown horse.

'All alone today?' he greeted her. 'No crazy horses or dogs?'

She smiled. 'No. Everybody and every animal seem to be otherwise occupied. I just felt I had to get away by myself for a while and think things over.'

'I saw you cross over the top. We'd just come in from a short ride, so I thought I'd catch you up. What's the matter? You look downcast. The Cannings been getting at you?'

'Only one of those grey days. I was feeling a bit miserable, so thought I'd try to walk it off.'

'It's not good to be alone at such times. Come on, jump up and have a ride.'

'Oh no.' Clare took a step backwards. 'I can't ride. I've never been on a horse.'

'You have to learn sometime, and what better time than now on Netty. She's the most gentle creature.' He swung down from his horse. 'Come on, I'll help you up.'

Clare looked down at her navy slacks — no reason why she shouldn't try. 'All right,' she said, 'but don't be surprised if I fall off.'

'You won't. Netty moves like an angel.'

He helped her up into the saddle of the smaller horse, gave her a few simple instructions, then remounted Rocket. For a while she felt strange then gradually settled down to the easy gait of her horse and enjoyed it. 'What upset you today?' he asked presently. 'Not like you to be so dispirited.'

'It was my own fault. I asked for it, being so curious. I asked Martha right out — insisted she tell me what happened at Moorlands, and what struck Penny dumb.'

'Oh!' His exclamation was expressive and he was silent for a long moment. 'It is never spoken of now, Clare. I don't really know much about it, as I told you — scandals don't seem to touch young boys. Young ones have problems and interests of their own.'

'Yes, I know. I wonder how many families never have an old skeleton in their cupboard?'

'That's the way. Don't let the Cannings pile their troubles on to you.'

'I've had troubles of my own, days of loneliness. It all came back today and I felt depressed.'

'But you feel better now?'

'Yes, I do.' She lifted her face to the sweet-scented air, unmarred by fumes or smoke. 'This is the way to see the moors.'

'You must ride again soon. When?'

She glanced up at him uncertainly. 'Not too soon. It isn't often I can get away alone.'

'This time, same day, next week.'

'All right, I'll try, but I can't promise.'

'You turn up, young lady, or I'll come for you.'

'No, oh no!' she cried, then seeing the smile on his face, knew he was teasing her. 'I don't want the Cannings to know — yet. They wouldn't understand.'

'We'll be discreet, but I don't mean to lose your friendship, so I'll look out for you.'

'Very well. Now I must be getting back.'

He turned at once and they drew up at about the same place as they had met, with the buildings of Hilltops high to their right. He helped her to dismount.

'That wasn't hard, was it? You've done very well.'

'I've enjoyed it very much. Thank you,' she said, her face warm with pleasure.

'Don't forget next week.'

'Well — '

He held up an admonishing finger and with a laugh she turned away and walked quickly back towards Moorlands. She couldn't help but like him and she was badly in need of friends. When he relaxed and smiled he was really a charming young man.

She turned up for her second riding lesson, of course, and it became quite a regular thing in time. From that it was a short step to going to Richard's home and meeting his people. There was Jess striding about the stables like a man, giving orders in her deep voice. It was a hive of activity there with all her horses and stable-boys, several of them going out periodically for a gallop over the moors. There was his older brother, Stephen, and a cousin of the same age, Malcolm. Also a comely, white-haired woman, Bertha, who had been with the family for at least thirty years, and probably knew more about their scandals than any of them put together. There was the mother and father, Bernard and Ada Layton, a quiet, pleasant couple, who had no time for the Cannings but welcomed Clare because she was a stranger to the moors and Richard liked her. They all worked hard and enjoyed their life. Martha had not called at Hilltops and Clare doubted if she ever would.

'I'm bound to be found out one day, you know,' Clare said to Richard, as they dismounted one sunny afternoon and sat for a while on some rocks amongst the heather. It was a high point on the moors, a favourite halting place of theirs. Not the wild place they had driven to some time ago, but with a fine view over the patchwork lands all the same, falling gently down to the thin church spire and clustered houses of Randgate. 'I had a job to get away today without Penny, and I think some of them are getting curious.'

'Does it matter? You wouldn't want to give this up now, would you?'

'No, but — ' she stared with a worried frown over the moors. 'I don't want to upset the Cannings. I like the life here and they took me in at face value. I'd hate to have to move on.'

'If they throw you out you can come to our place, Clare, so stop worrying about it.'

She looked up at him, the dark, bronze-streaked hair tumbled about his forehead, and smiled. 'That makes me feel better.' She put up a hand and stroked Netty's brown flank as the horse nosed against her shoulder. 'It's a lovely change horse-riding. I've never been one for a car really, except for getting quickly from place to place.'

'Like Jess. She never uses a car if she can help it, and I don't blame her. She's got the right idea.'

'You think a lot of her, don't you?'

He pondered a moment. 'I suppose we all wait on her word. You might say she is a forceful character. I think we'd perhaps drift apart without her. She's the one who sees opportunities and seizes them, who takes a gamble and it usually pays off.'

'Such as Cannings' land — '

'Yes, of course. Immediately they came on the market.'

Jess should have been a man, thought Clare not for the first time. So full of energy and determination, strong-willed, driving them all before her, and strong in body.

After a while of blissful silence, Richard said, 'Clare, some friends of ours are having a barn dance on Saturday. Some sort of celebration. I'd like you to go with me, will you?'

Clare hesitated. 'I'd love to go but — Richard, could we take Penny with us?'

'No,' he said quickly. 'Just you, Clare.' As she frowned, he said, 'You do enough for them, and you are with Penny most days of the week. You must live your own life away from them sometimes.'

She sighed. 'I can't help feeling sorry for Penny. Seventeen and so little fun in her life. All right, Richard, I'd love to go. I haven't danced for ages. I'll drive over and we'll go in my car.'

'Fine.' His eyes glowed warmly. 'I'll expect you about six o'clock.'

The men had been shearing sheep that week and were tired, and they looked surprised when Clare said on Saturday that she would be going to a dance that night near Randgate.

'Was it advertised?' asked Martha suspiciously.

'No, I've been invited. It's at someone's farm, someone called Deacon.' Clare waited for them to ask more, but as they didn't she left them wondering.

Only Timothy said, 'Gettin' to know folks, ain't you?'

'She gets about more than we do, with her car and shopping and all,' said Martha.

They appeared satisfied with that, and early that evening Clare donned a pretty soft-pink, summer dress and a light coat, then set out in her car for Hilltops.

The dance was in a big empty barn, cleared of everything but a long trestle table for refreshments, and a space for the four local boys' band. It was apparently a celebration for the birth of twins to the Deacon family, and an iced cake ringed with bottles and glasses stood in the centre of the table. Everybody was jolly and friendly, and Clare was accepted as though she had lived there for years.

'I never thought I'd get this far with you, Clare,' Richard said, as they waltzed together, his chin brushing her curly head.

'No.' She laughed. 'It's amazing, isn't it?'

'Remember the first day we met? Whatever made me so disagreeable with you?'

'And the time after that and the time after that. You'd decided I was tainted with the Canning blood, I suppose.'

'Well, yes, I thought you were related

or something, and we'd had quite a load of trouble from Cannings one way and another. That mare had trodden down our vegetation more than once, you know.'

'She's got her eye on Rocket, I think.'

'You could be right there. They'd be a pair, those two. What are you laughing at?'

'Some day I'll tell you, perhaps. Just now I'm remembering you glaring at me, as though you'd like to horsewhip me for going in the copse. Both of us behaving like silly children. Those bluebells!'

'We'd had an anonymous letter that day accusing us of some mad thing. It could only have come from Cannings.'

She shook her head, her laughter dying. 'Oh no, I'm sure they'd never stoop to that.'

'Well, I hope not. Some trouble-maker, I suppose, knowing the bad feeling between us. But it made me bad-tempered and I vented my anger on you.'

It was quite late that evening when Clare saw that Louis was there. Looking more handsome and debonair than ever in a dark suit and immaculate shirt. 'Oh dear,' she said, trying to hide behind Richard. 'That's torn it.'

'What's the matter?'

'Louis, our farm-hand, is here. It will get back to the Cannings now.'

'Don't let it worry you. He might think it's none of their business, and you are free to go where you like, anyway.'

Louis had noticed her almost at once, though, and he came over to her when the next dance started. A quickstep, and he took the chance to hold her to him tightly. She tried to draw back from the smell of hair-oil mingling with his beer-laden breath.

'Loosen up, Louis. I can hardly breathe.'

'It's too warm in here. Going to be a storm, I guess.'

'You've been drinking. Don't hold me so tightly, Louis, or I won't dance with you any more.'

'Can't be nice to me, can you?' His face leered close to hers. 'Not good enough for you, eh? It'd be a different thing if Richard Layton was holding you like this, wouldn't it?'

'Don't be ridiculous — '

'Oh, I've seen you two together in different places, so you can't cod me. But I'd make you a much better lover than he would. I've taken a fancy to you, didn't you know that?'

His lips brushed her ear and she strove to break his close hold. 'I don't want you — or any fellow. You're drunk, Louis,' she said again, 'or you'd never say such things. Now dance properly or I'm going to sit down.'

His grip slackened. 'What's Joseph Canning going to say if I tell him you're knocking around with the Layton chap?'

'Tell him if you like,' said Clare, exasperated. She had not liked Louis from the start, distrusting him, and how right she had been! 'I can leave here whenever I wish. I'm not beholden to any of them and I'll go tomorrow if I feel like it. It was only unforeseen circumstances that kept me here in the first place.'

'Oh, don't go.' His tone changed. 'It was a miserable place before you came — don't know how I stuck it. Joseph bad-tempered — and Martha, come to that — ordering us about. All of them with long faces. A dreary old place. So don't go, Miss Clare.'

The music stopped and there was a beeline to the table for refreshments. 'Please don't go,' he urged again.

'All right, but it's up to you, Louis,' she said quietly, glad to be free of him at last and determined that would be the last dance he would have with her! 'Tell them anything you want, but let's have no more nonsense. I can choose my own friends whether you or other people like them or not.'

He stared into her unsmiling face then went away. Jess Layton came towards her. The woman wore a white silk shirt with a tie and tight, slim slacks, and Clare guessed there would be a horse waiting somewhere outside for her.

'Has that wife-beater been annoying you? You looked furious with him,' said Jess.

'Wife-beater?' gasped Clare. 'He has a wife?'

'He had. Divorced. I don't know about beating her, but he gave the poor girl a hell of a time. He has a cruel streak in him and I wouldn't trust him an inch.'

'Neither would I. I've always felt that.'

'Good. Keep him at a distance is my advice. He's a handsome devil and a hit with some of the women, but he's unreliable. A double-crosser.'

'How did he come to be employed by Joseph Canning? If he's all you say he is, he's hardly the type to appeal to them.'

'Well, I take it that he puts on a good show up there. He's a good farmer and if he does his work well, I don't think Joseph is one to question him much about his private life.'

'That's true,' murmured Clare. Hadn't they taken her in on trust and given her the run of the house without references or questions of any kind? Only old Timothy had wondered where she had come from, but simply because he was naturally inquisitive — and even he had taken to her on the spot.

'Richard tells me you haven't met Dora Walters yet,' said Jess, breaking into her musing. 'Here she is. Dora, this is Miss Clare Bowers.'

The tall attractive woman came up and took Clare's hand. 'Hello! You're at the farm, Moorlands, aren't you?'

'Yes, I'm living there for a while.' Clare met the clear grey eyes, unembarrassed. 'I was bound for Scotland some months ago but got held up here. I liked it so much I decided to stay for a while.'

'So you like it here? Who doesn't?' Clare felt the woman was taking in every detail of her short curly hair, trim figure and pretty light dress. 'Joseph has told me about you.'

'Has he?' said Clare, surprised.

'Yes. He seems well satisfied with the arrangement.' Dora Walters was smiling. Evidently, even if she were jealous of Clare's vantage point in the Canning household, she had no intention of showing it.

'And well-fed, too, I hope,' said Clare, with a laugh. 'That seems to be the general idea of me staying. Head-cook and bottle-washer.'

'How long are you staying? They'll miss you if you go.'

'I've no plans yet, Mrs. Walters, but I suppose I'll move on one of these days,' said Clare, her eyes on Richard's dark head as he advanced towards them.

'Oh, do call me Dora,' said the other, turning to help herself to some sandwiches. 'Everybody does.'

At last the party was over and Clare and Richard came out to the heavy warm night. 'You drive till we get to

126

Hilltops,' she said. 'I've gone suddenly tired.'

She sank low in the seat beside him and as he drove down the road towards Lambreck, he glanced down at her. 'Have you enjoyed it?' he asked, his voice soft and caressing.

'Yes, very much. Thank you for taking me, Richard.' She moved away from his shoulder, hoping he was not going to start being amorous. She liked him a great deal, but what with Louis and his words still rankling, she did not feel like coping with any more of that sort of thing.

'It's been great having you with me tonight, Clare,' he said. 'I don't know what I've done all this time without you.' He looked down at her again but her eyes were closed. He smiled and shrugged and drove on faster. Clare kept her eyes closed, feeling sweet relief in the warm summer air wafting through the open window. It was easier that way.

Richard got out at the bottom of the

lane leading to Moorlands and she drove on, soon drawing slowly into the open barn of the farm. She closed the gates and entered the house quietly. They would all have been in bed long ago, she thought. Only Sam was there in the kitchen, raising his head from the hearthrug and thumping his tail.

They were not all in bed, however. As she made for the stairs, Joseph came out of the seldom-used sitting-room.

7

'You're back, then,' Joseph said, as she stared in surprise. His shirt was open to the waist, exposing his broad, ginger-haired chest, and there were ink-stains on his fingers.

'Yes. It has been so nice. You're late to bed, Joseph.'

'It's awfully close. I couldn't sleep, so I came down to do some book work.'

Through the open door Clare could see the big old desk littered with papers. Joseph hated any desk-work and business papers, and only put his mind to it when it became really essential.

'You look very pretty tonight,' he said, his eyes on her flimsy dress.

'Joseph,' said Clare impulsively, conscience pricking her, 'some of the Laytons were there.'

'Were they?' He was silent a long

moment. 'That's not surprising.'

'I think you ought to know that I often see Richard Layton and sometimes the others. I've been horse-riding with them, too.'

'I know.' He nodded gravely. 'Father told me. He saw you.'

That old man! thought Clare in amazement. He misses nothing. 'I'm sorry I haven't mentioned it sooner, and I hope you don't mind, Joseph. They have been so kind to me. They never call this family — otherwise I'd have nothing to do with them.'

'It's all right, Clare. What you do is your own affair, but I'm glad you've told me.'

'If it displeases you I'll leave here and move on to fresh fields!'

'No, of course not, though I'm sorry they've got hold of you. I've no time for those people, so just you be careful. I wouldn't want you to be hurt by those Laytons.'

She stared up into his grave face, disturbed that she had gone against his wishes yet reluctant to lose Richard's friendship.

'Do as you like, Clare, don't worry about us, but be careful and keep Penny away from them, that's all.' A faint smile crossed his lips. 'Now, good night. I'm glad you've enjoyed the evening. Off to bed with you.'

She smiled at him, not knowing how to express her relief that he had taken it so well. Thank goodness she had mentioned it, as he already knew. Continual deceit would have robbed her of the friendliness at Moorlands. He turned back into the sitting-room and she went up the stairs.

The thunderstorm prophesied by Louis arrived, but not till the following afternoon when Clare was returning from a stroll over the moors with Laddie. Somewhere near there was a shepherd's stone hut, and she hurried onwards against the driving rain, with lightning slashing through the black clouds and thunder echoing round the hills, hoping she was travelling in the right direction. Her wet clothes already clinging to her limbs, she stumbled at last through the doorless opening of the hut, then was startled to see two other people sheltering there. A couple clasped in each other's arms. Penny — of all people — and Terry Grant!

'Oh, sorry!' Clare said, dashing rain water from her eyes, then, 'Oh, Laddie!' — as the dog shook himself vigorously, spraying them all with water.

'It's all right,' Terry said quietly. 'Penny is afraid of lightning.' Even as he spoke lightning flashed through the dim enclosure again and Penny cringed against him.

'I'm glad she's not out alone in it,' said Clare, then feeling idiotic because they were speaking of Penny instead of to her, as so often happened. She leant up against the wall, trying to dry her neck and face with an already damp handkerchief. There was nowhere to sit except on the rough earth floor.

After a few moments as the storm seemed to ease a little, Terry said, 'I think you ought to know, Clare, that I love Penny — very much, and I think she loves me.'

Penny looked up and smiled at Clare, nodding eagerly.

'I'm glad to hear that, but — ' Clare hesitated. What about the other girls? As his grandmother said, could this nice-looking young man be sure of himself yet, know his own mind? 'Penny is very young yet.'

'We're going to get married, aren't we, Penny love?' Again another nod, and the girl turned her flushed face into his shoulder.

'You're going to find it rather difficult, I'm afraid, Terry — I mean Penny's father,' Clare added hastily, 'I'm all for it, but her father keeps a watchful eye on her. She is only seventeen. You'll have to wait.'

'Oh, we'll wait a year and that's quite long enough. It won't make any difference, will it, Penny? No one is going to keep us apart.'

'You'll have to get them accustomed

to it slowly, and you need to make them understand, Penny, that you want to be with Terry more than anything. Your father will have to realise how things are going — that he'll have to part with you one day.'

'It won't be as though we'll be going far away,' said Terry.

Penny held out her hand and clung warmly to Clare as the other took it and said, 'You know I'll do all I can to help, Penny. Your father has had a sad life and we can't blame him. We must be patient.'

They were silent for a while, then Clare went to the doorway and looked at the brightening sky. Thunder rumbled in the distance.

'I think the storm is about over, so I'll be on my way now. Don't be too late in, Penny. Goodbye, both of you. Come, Laddie.'

'Well, fancy that!' mused Clare, skirting puddles, with tall wet grasses swishing at her calves — but it was no real surprise. She hoped Terry would prove trustworthy. It would be wonderful for Penny, and he seemed to understand and protect her as much as anybody.

As she might have expected, Joseph saw her approaching and waited for her. 'I thought Penny was with you,' he said.

'I've seen her. She'll be along soon. She's with Terry, Joseph.'

He frowned. 'You should have persuaded her to come back with you,' he said coolly. 'You know my feelings about that.'

'They think a lot of each other,' she said boldly. 'You'll have to get used to it, I'm afraid.'

He shook his head. 'No.'

'Joseph, why don't you clear the remains of that old fire away?' she said, abruptly changing the subject, as they passed the ugly debris of the destroyed barn. 'I'm sure the ground would be useful to you, and it would be much better for Penny. She is frightened of that spot.'

'She is?' His eyebrows lifted in surprise. Could it be he had never noticed? 'Then she must remember something of that time.'

'I'm quite sure she does.'

'To please you I'll have it scraped clean, then.' He moved away and over his shoulder said wryly, 'Martha can build more stables there for her future racehorses.' Turning from a barn door he looked back again and said, 'Go and get those wet things off. You look drenched.'

At last she had achieved something if she had managed to influence him to clear away that horrid reminder of the past. He was an obstinate, severe man, but he had his amiable moments after all, it seemed. It would be better for his own peace of mind, too, to have the ruins swept away and something useful put in its place.

Clare felt easier for telling Joseph about her friendship with the Hilltops people, and went for her rides out with Richard, and sometimes Jess, regularly.

She took to visiting their farm, as well, always welcomed warmly by homely Bernard Layton and his wife. Yet a time must come when she would have to leave, if for no other reason than that she was getting too fond of Richard, and she felt sure he was of her. He would meet her every day if she permitted it, and he had taken to lifting her down bodily from her horse, his arms firmly about her. Last time he had bent low over her face, his lips near, his blue eyes smiling deep into hers. She had laughed and turned away.

'I ought to be able to dismount by myself now,' she said.

'I don't want you falling on your nose and knocking your face about again.'

'I must have looked a sight that day I fell through the hedge.'

He caught hold of her hand. 'I'm glad it happened. I've never been so happy as I've been since that day.'

'And I'm glad I came here and met you all. Come along, let's go and see what Jess is doing with that pony.'

Leading Rocket and Netty they went down towards what Jess called the 'round field'. It was a natural circus-ring with short crisp turf and bordered by low hedges and the remains of an ancient wall. Jess, holding the reins, was running round with a smart young brown pony, newly-saddled, tossing his head with enjoyment. Suddenly Jess drew him to a halt and sank to the grass, breathless. The pony ducked his head and nudged her shoulder.

'He's great, isn't he? Great!' she exclaimed.

'Has he a name?' asked Clare.

'Of course. He's Bellboy, one of Belle's infants.'

'How you adore your horses!' said Clare. She stared down at Jess lolling there. A well-made woman, strong throat and chin rising from a blue-checked open-necked shirt. She was no beauty as women went, but she would have made an attractive man. As the pony came to her Clare smoothed her hand over its velvety nose and ears.

'And I'm beginning to understand why. They are beautiful creatures.'

'How is Martha Canning coping?' asked Jess.

'She seems quite happy, but I wish she would come to see you. I'm sure she needs someone. The men leave so much organising to her.'

Yet, thought Clare, Martha was unconsciously shaping herself in the image of Jess Layton. She had started leaving off aprons and skirts and taken to shabby slacks and washed-out blouses — more suitable for 'hauling animals about' she said. Then one day, to Clare's astonishment, she came to her with a large pair of scissors.

'Here, Clare, cut this off for me.' She dropped her long hair down her back. 'It's too much bother, always dropping about my ears when I'm busy.'

Clare laughed and took the scissors. 'Well, I'm no expert at this, you know.'

'You cut your own.'

'It's simple being curly. I just cut lumps off when they get in the way. It doesn't matter, anyway. We're not moving in high society.'

'That's true. So carry on, please.'

Clare seized the long mane and cut. After a while Martha said, 'Shorter, Clare. Take this off' — holding up the side pieces of the bob length — 'Cut it short like — well, very much shorter.'

'Like Jess Layton' she had almost said. Smiling to herself, Clare carefully trimmed the hair to the neat head.

'Goodness, Martha, you should have done this before,' she said, going in front to look at the other woman with the rusty-coloured grey-streaked hair. 'You look years younger. It suits you.'

'Never mind that. It's comfort I'm after. I'm no beauty and nothing will change that, and I'll have no need of this again.' Martha got up quickly and picked up her discarded switch of hair.

'Martha!' — but before Clare could say anything else the hair was flung into the back of the perpetually glowing red fire and was at once a sizzling, smelling wad.

'Well, I suppose you can always grow it again,' said Clare.

'That I will not. We've been behind the times far too long at this place.'

'Good lord!' ejaculated Joseph, when he saw Martha that evening. He looked aghast, angry for a moment, no doubt also sensing the likeness to Jess Layton, then he turned away.

'Now I'm back with the animals, Joe,' said Martha. 'It's got on my nerves dropping all over the place when I'm bending and stooping.'

'That's all right. You've aways done things your own way without asking me, but don't you dare cut off any of Penny's hair.'

'Of course not,' Clare put in quickly, thinking of that lustrous auburn hair falling each side of Penny's lovely face. 'She looks right as she is, and I'm sure she likes it that way herself.'

'Penny is old enough to please herself,' said Martha, in her brief, sharp manner. 'In more ways than one. Here she comes now, holding hands with that Grant boy.'

Joseph scowled and made a move for the door. Clare took a chance. This could ruin everything for Penny. 'Be careful with her, Joseph. She's very happy and I'm certain you can trust Terry.'

He stared back at her coldly, a retort on his lips, then shook his head and came back into the room. 'She is all that matters to me.'

'Then you wouldn't want to see her unhappy.'

He shook his big head again. 'Things have changed since you came here, Clare,' he said, his eyes on his sister's clipped hair.

'Don't blame Clare for this,' said Martha, pushing a hand up through her hair. 'I've been damned sick of it flopping about. As for Penny — if you weren't so blind to all that goes on around here you'd have seen this happening long ago.'

Joseph looked back at Clare. 'We've cleared away most of that rubble today,' he said, and went away across the narrow hall into the sitting-room. The door shut smartly behind him.

Terry and Penny came in hesitantly. 'Sit down, Terry. We're just about to get some tea, aren't we, Martha?' said Clare. Penny was staring in amazement at her aunt. 'Do you like it, Penny? Martha was tired of her old bun.'

The girl suddenly smiled, leapt across the room and embraced Martha with every sign of excitement and pleasure.

'There, see?' laughed Clare. 'We all think you look a smasher, Martha.'

'Oh, go on with you!' scoffed the older woman, but she looked pleased and younger for her hair-cut and exhilaration.

One day some time later, as Clare came out of a shop in Randgate and went towards her car, her arms full of parcels, she walked right into Dora Walters.

'Hello, Miss Bowers.' Dora eyed the

parcels. 'You do a lot for the Cannings. They'll miss you when you go.'

'I think I only stay for Penny's and Martha's sake,' said Clare. 'I'm sorry for Martha, she hates housework, but Penny helps me and is learning to cook now. I think Martha kept her out of the kitchen before.'

'They always treat her as though she's made of spun glass. So you have no further plans yet?' asked the other quietly.

'No, not yet.' Clare turned from dropping her purchases into the car. 'I'll run you back home if you're ready.'

'Would you?' The woman smiled. 'It will save me so much time, waiting for the bus. Thank you very much.'

'I don't think you will ever leave here,' said Dora, when Clare pulled up outside her narrow little cottage shortly afterwards. 'You seem quite settled.'

'I've certainly taken to it, but I'm afraid — for certain reasons — I'll have to move on one day.'

'Come in for a cup of tea. I've never

144

had much chance of getting to know you.'

Clare followed her through the door with its brass knocker into an oblong room. Dora went into an adjoining room to put the kettle on. Tea turned up with home-made scones and jam and a sponge cake as light as thistledown. There was a long bookcase full of interesting books, and everywhere shone clean and cared-for. Here was a woman who was a good cook and who enjoyed her house.

As Clare pondered yet again why Joseph did not marry this attractive, competent woman, Dora said, 'Will you ask Joseph to call round sometime? I haven't seen him for weeks.'

Clare looked up. Dora's face had changed, suddenly devoid of light. Before she had time to force a smile Clare saw misery there. Without a doubt this woman wanted Joseph, and secretly envied Clare's sway over them at Moorlands, blaming her for Joseph's absence.

'I'll tell him,' Clare said, then impulsively — 'Why don't you set out to get him, Dora, if you care about him? I'm sure he needs someone.'

'He thinks a lot of you.'

'Oh, I wouldn't say that. Only as a new interest, a new housekeeper. Grateful perhaps because I'm kind to Penny.'

'Ah! Anyone who takes on Joseph takes on Penny, too. She's a delightful child, of course — '

'She is no longer a child. Another year and she'll probably be married herself. Dumbness doesn't make her incapable, and she has a lively mind.'

'Married?'

'Terry Grant.'

'Oh, of course.'

'If I felt you had a foot at last in that household, Dora, I'd move on.'

'You don't care, then — about Joseph — ' asked Dora carefully.

'I'll hate to go, but not because of him.'

'Well, we'll see. Thank you for — '

being so frank, Clare.'

Clare laughed lightly. 'I say too much sometimes, and it nearly lands me in trouble.'

When at last she rose to go, Dora put a hand on her arm. 'I hope we'll stay good friends, Clare. I like you.'

'Yes, whatever happens, we'll stay friends, I hope,' said Clare. If only this kind woman knew how much she needed the support and comfort of friends!

That evening, catching Joseph alone as he scalded out churns in the long cool dairy, Clare ventured, 'I met Dora again today, Joseph, and she wonders why she hasn't seen you for so long. She wants you to call.'

He looked surprised, then shrugged. 'It's a busy time. She ought to know that.'

'You ought to have some time off, though, Joseph.'

'Dora knows where I am if she wants me.' As Clare turned away, lost for words, he said coolly, 'Don't you start

147

getting at me like Father and Martha. I'm quite satisfied with things as they are.'

'Here I am interfering again. I'm sorry, Joseph — it's just that Dora wanted me to ask you. I like her and she seemed so disappointed.'

'All right, Clare. I'll look in on her next time I'm down in the village.'

'Thank you. I wish you would.' Clare went back to the house. Well, she had done her best about Dora, she thought. It was up to the other woman now. The churns clattered about noisily behind her, as though Joseph were venting his feelings on them. It was time she packed her bag and left, the way she seemed to be getting more and more involved with the people here. Yet she dreaded leaving, with the prospect of facing a friendless, lonely life in a new place once more. She would miss them all, even the animals — and above anything else, of course, Richard Layton.

8

Clare was in the kitchen, about a week later, when a shabby car jolted into the cobbled yard. She waited, listening, hoping Martha or one of the others would be on hand to attend to whoever it was. She had no time for strangers, and she was more than usually worried because they had driven straight into the yard instead of stopping at the gates. There were voices, a man's, a high-pitched woman's and a child's voice.

'Nobody here as usual — ' said the man. There were heavy footsteps across the kitchen's flagged floor and he came into the inner room, confronting an alarmed Clare.

'Well, well,' he said. 'Who are you?'

Clare, propped up against the table, drew herself up to her full height. 'A friend. I help Martha — do the cooking.'

'A home-help. Well, well,' he said again. 'I wonder how long *you'll* stay here?'

'I've been here since early spring. I'm quite happy here.'

He eyed her critically for a moment. 'I'd say they were fortunate to find someone like you. I'm Joseph's brother, Gilbert. I suppose they're all out somewhere.'

He was fair-haired, not as ruddy as his brother, but just as tall and broad, and now she could see his likeness to the rest of the family.

'They're getting the last of the hay in,' she said.

'Not the old man, too? I thought he was past it.'

'Mr. Timothy will be in the garden somewhere, I expect. He's quite well except for his backache at times.'

'Never alters, this place, does it? Always behind the times, still in the same old rut.' He looked with distaste at the plain kitchen with its bare, scored table, shallow sink and shelves of blackened pans.

'Martha is working hard to improve things and I think she is making headway,' said Clare stoutly.

'Well, I can see they have a champion in you, whoever you are. Joseph lacks spirit — our old man has more go in him.' He turned to the door as the woman's shrill voice called him. 'But how such a good-looker as you happens to be here, heaven knows.'

'Gilbert, where are you?' came the querulous voice again. 'I want you to get the luggage in. I'm hot and tired and want to change.' A tall thin woman with thick dark hair and good-looking but sharp features, a petulant mouth, appeared in the doorway.

'My wife, Thelma,' said the man, 'and somewhere there's our daughter, Sandra. Eleven. She'll be up the yard poking her nose into something, I expect. A born fidget. Thelma, this is — er — '

'Clare,' came the answer. 'I help with the housekeeping.'

'Would it be asking too much, then,

for a cup of tea?' asked the other woman. 'I feel lousy. Travelling always makes my head ache.'

'It will be ready in a minute,' said Clare, reaching for cups and saucers.

'I'm hoping they can put us up for a time,' said Gilbert. 'Is my old room still unoccupied, I wonder?'

'Well, I'm in the room at the far end — '

'That was my other sisters' room, so it looks as though mine will still be vacant. The one opposite the bathroom, and there should be a small one nearby for Sandra.'

Too many bedrooms, Clare had so often thought. Yet once years ago they had been full of life, ringing with the voices of Timothy and his wife and all their sons and daughters.

'I'll see that the beds are made for you presently,' she said. 'They'll be surprised to see you here, no doubt.'

He laughed grimly. 'That they will! Not too pleased about it, either, I can promise you.'

When she carried the tray in Clare found that they had made themselves at home. Gilbert was in the rocking-chair and his wife slumped in the chair opposite, her high-heeled shoes flung off.

A girl with fair hair swinging about her face came in. She had sharp features like her mother, making her look older than she really was. Close behind came Penny, looking confused and unhappy. Clare knew the signs and longed to take her in her arms and comfort her.

'She won't talk to me,' declared the younger girl. 'Even when I pinched her she won't talk. She's daft.'

'Penny can't talk,' said Clare, taking a dislike to the child at once and wanting to shake her. 'She was ill and her voice won't work, so don't worry her. She can't talk.'

'Well, she's daft. Who are you?'

'I'm Clare. Sit down and have some tea. Would you like biscuits or cake?'

'Both.'

'Sandra, mind your manners,' said Gilbert lazily.

Through the window Clare saw a load of hay swinging into the yard. 'Penny dear, go and see if that's your father and bring him here, will you?' Anything to get disturbed Penny away from these people and give her time to become accustomed to any change, and if Joseph were there to help all the better for herself.

Penny, looking decidedly relieved, ran out at once. A few minutes later Joseph strode in, worried by his daughter's urgent signs.

'What are *you* doing here?' he demanded, frowning, his eyes passing from his brother to the gloomy-faced woman, then to the child stuffing cake into her mouth.

Gilbert got up but did not proffer his hand. Evidently the brothers had little affection for each other, thought Clare.

'To come to the point, I'm asking for shelter for a time. The firm's closed down — I'm on my beam ends,' said

154

Gilbert, staring at Joseph boldly.

'I might have known it. You've never been any good, have you, Gilbert? If you think you're going to heap yourself and your family on us — '

'You can't turn him away,' said Timothy's voice from the outer doorway. 'He's our own flesh and blood, and he needs help.'

'Hello, Father,' said Gilbert glibly. 'Glad to see you still getting around.'

'He always sucks up to you, Father,' said Joseph angrily. 'He wants it all easy. The times you've helped him!'

'Where can he come but to his old home? You'll have to let him stay a few weeks while he gets back into work again.' The old man walked past Gilbert, nodding to Thelma as he passed, took possession of his rocking-chair and picked up his pipe.

'All right,' Joseph said. 'Stay if you must — but I hope you're going to get stuck into it and earn your keep. We're short-handed. A pity you couldn't think to come in time for the haymaking, but not you, oh no.'

'I didn't give it a thought,' said Gilbert leisurely, stretching his long arms.

'Well, there's still plenty to do, so the sooner you start the better. And keep your child away from the little barn. There's a sick cow in there.'

'Not very hospitable, are you?' muttered Gilbert. 'Still the same stony-faced Joe.'

'This is your last chance, mind,' put in Timothy. 'A few weeks only, not a lifetime. You can't blame Joe.'

'And another thing,' said Joseph. 'Get your wife to pull her weight. Clare is only a friend helping us out — not a paid skivvy for us all. She's not going to run around waiting on you. Understand?'

'Only too well,' said Gilbert, with a meaning wink at Clare.

'And treat her with respect. Keep your dirty tongue in your head.' Joseph glared at his brother as though he would strike him, then turned on his heel and went out, slamming the door behind him.

'You'd better keep on the right side of Joe,' said Timothy, puffing a red glow into his pipe at last. 'He's had more than enough to put up with, and you've never put your back into it as he has. Is there any more tea in that pot, Clare?'

'Of course there is.' Clare went to get a cup for him, glad to be on the move, and wishing she had thought to thrust a mug of heart-warming liquid into Joseph's hand.

'Grandpa,' said Sandra, 'People who can't talk are daft babies, aren't they?'

'No, they are not.' Timothy rocked his chair violently. 'They are much nicer than those who talk too much, with their mouth full, too.'

'How can they tell us anything?'

'They are more brainy than chatter-boxes. They think a lot more, and if you're meaning our Penny, you'd better mind what you say, young lady. She knows an awful lot, does Penny.'

Sandra muttered something, unconvinced, but the old man did not appear to hear. Penny had not returned and Clare went to find her, leaving Gilbert to sort things out with his father. She found the girl down by the stables, watching Martha mixing some food for the animals. She put an arm about Penny's shoulders.

'Penny dear, don't let that child worry you,' she murmured. 'Martha,' she said, raising her voice, 'your brother Gilbert, his wife and daughter are here.'

Martha nodded. 'Aye, so Joe told me. Damn it, as though we haven't enough on our plates without them hanging around. They are both bone-idle, Gilbert hates farm-life, and he always rubs Joe up the wrong way.'

'It's only for two or three weeks.'

'And that's far too long.' Martha frowned heavily, looking a great deal like her brother Joseph in that moment.

'You're lucky to have someone like Clare,' Gilbert said, as they sat at their evening meal.

'So we are,' said Joseph dryly. 'A very nice arrangement while she decides to stay here.'

'I can't understand a place like this appealing to a young pretty woman.'

'But then you always hated the life here, didn't you? You only come back to it when you've nowhere else to go.'

'I think the moors are beautiful,' said Clare. 'I like the peace and freshness of it all.'

'Then you are no city girl.' Clare knew he had been staring at her for some time. She looked up suddenly and met his rather prominent grey eyes. 'But it's really odd,' he went on. 'I seem to have seen you somewhere before, and I can't think where.'

A shiver passed through Clare, but she forced herself to go on with her meal calmly. 'It's hardly likely,' she said. 'And I've certainly never met you before.'

'I'd swear I've seen you some-where — '

'I led a really quiet life, rarely went

159

anywhere, so I still say it's impossible.'

'Let the girl be,' interrupted Timothy. 'You're always coming up with some crazy notion.'

Clare smiled at the old man gratefully. She was conscious of Sandra devouring food at her side. She was a vulgar, greedy eater. Her mother was absent, having gone to her room and pleading her headache.

The weeks following were anything but easy for any of them. The peaceful, orderly routine of the farmhouse was disrupted, and everybody seemed miserable. Thelma spent most of the mornings in bed and littered the bathroom with her fancy toilet requisites, trailing damp towels about the place. She did hardly anything to help Clare, studying with care her thin pale hands, but Clare said nothing, preferring the woman's absence to her company. Yet she knew Joseph was bound to notice before long.

The sitting-room was in an untidy state, as the newcomers seemed to have taken almost complete possession of it. Joseph was furiously angry when he found his desk disarrayed and that Sandra had taken his writing-paper to scribble on. Gilbert's work about the farm was erratic. More often than not he was off somewhere in his old car, with the pretext of looking for work when Joseph challenged him.

Penny was miserable and disappeared whenever she could, taking her puppy, Honey, with her. Sandra baited her and tormented the puppy, and the easiest way, when Clare was not with her, was to make off to a secret nook somewhere or down to Terry's home. Sandra was a pest, Clare told herself. The girl searched for eggs and broke several. She climbed apple trees and was ill afterwards with gorging too much of the fruit. She pulled peas and beans ruthlessly off Timothy's plants and climbed barbed wire, tearing clothes and scratching herself.

'She ought to have been a boy,' said Gilbert, with a queer sort of pride. They had no control over their wayward child.

Clare tried new tactics. She handed Sandra a basket and asked her to collect some eggs, and as she had hoped the ruse worked. Because Sandra thought Clare would be pleased if she got the eggs, she lost all interest in them, also in the peas and other small tasks requested of her.

Clare tried to keep an eye on Penny, because Sandra could be cruel, and the older girl so sensitive and vulnerable. So one day when Joseph's daughter had been missing for much longer than usual and there was no sign of Sandra, either, she went in search of her. Penny was not in any of her usual haunts and she'd had no intention of visiting Terry's grandmother that day. Neither Dan nor Martha knew where she was, but the latter suddenly remembered she had seen Penny going along to the far end of the buildings, towards the storage barn. Louis had been following, talking to her. Fear shook Clare.

'Louis!' she gasped.

'I expect he was taking her to see an injured bird they've brought in from the fields,' said Martha offhandedly.

There must be some reason for Penny to stay with Louis. He had persuaded her to go along with him, and only an injured bird or something similar would arouse her interest, as usually she was nervous of Louis and avoided him when possible. Clare took to her heels and ran all the way to the little-used barn. It was cobwebby and dark and never entered except for occasional tools or spare parts. Its corners were cluttered with dusty, discarded bits of machinery and broken cart-wheels, and straw was strewn about its dusty floor.

'Penny!' Clare called. 'Where are you?'

She was about to return, thinking the girl must have gone up over the moors after all, when she heard a scuffling noise inside the old barn. She pushed at the door and found it difficult to open.

'Penny, are you there?' she cried.

The scrambling inside became more pronounced. She kicked at the door, threw her whole weight against it, but at last it grated open enough for her to squeeze through. It smelt dusty and hot inside, and there was a wild struggle going on towards the back. Her eyes growing used to the dimness she saw Penny on the floor, fighting madly in the arms of Louis. Her clothes were torn, her face was scratched, she kicked and clawed violently, but her eyes were wide with terror and her gaping mouth sound-lessly crying for help.

'Louis, leave Penny alone! Let her go at once!' Clare clutched at his shoul-ders, trying to drag him away. 'What do you think you are doing? Leave her alone at once!'

Holding Penny down firmly by her shoulders and the weight of his body, he leered up at Clare. 'You go away and mind your own business. If you had more time for me I would leave her alone, see? But as it is — ' he bent and forced his lips over Penny's mouth.

Clare looked around helplessly, suddenly snatched up a heavy rake. 'Let her go at once or else — '

He glanced up at her again, his face changing. 'Have some sense! You wouldn't — '

'Let her go or you'll get this!' Clare raised the rake menacingly.

He realised at last that Clare was angry enough to do anything. He released Penny, who crawled up into a huddle, shaking with soundless sobs, and got to his feet.

'All right, you win. I've been a fool — I never thought — '

'Stay where you are — don't come near me — ' as he moved towards her. The prongs of the rake swayed dangerously towards his face. Clare's lips were tight, her expression fearless and determined, her own troubled life in the past having hardened her so that she felt capable of anything. He stood still.

'So now I suppose you'll be telling Joseph?'

'I want you to leave here at once. Tell Joseph you are leaving for good. If you don't I certainly will tell him about this.'

'It won't happen again. I was mad to touch the girl, but there's been no harm done.'

'If you stay here Penny will be terrified every time she sees you — and I'd never trust you again, either. Look what you've done to her — no harm indeed! Her torn dress — the state she's in. Keep back, Louis' — the rake swayed forward — 'or this will spoil your good looks. You'll have to go. Otherwise I'll tell Joseph — and he'll just about kill you.'

He pulled a long face. 'He would at that. He's not going to be so gentle about me walking out on him, either, leaving him short-handed.'

'His brother will have to do more. Now get out of my sight, and the sooner you leave the better.'

He tried more half-hearted persuasion, but knew he had met his match in this hot-tempered, determined, little-known woman. He raised his hands with a hopeless gesture, then turned to the door.

'This place isn't much loss, anyway.' He dragged the door open with an ill-tempered heave, then glared back at her, hating her in those last minutes. 'But you'll pay for this, Miss Smarty Clare. Somehow I'll make you pay for this!'

'Clear out, Louis!' Her tone was urgent, icy, but cold shivers chased up and down her back. Could he get his revenge? What could he do or find out about her? The time was surely drawing near when she would have to depart from this part of the country, before she had to make any explanations. Would they believe her any more than the others? Louis would always remember her that day with the ugly rake raised high, the hot anger in her face.

She put the rake down and drew

Penny to her feet, enfolding her in her arms, as Louis's footsteps died away. The girl clutched at her brokenheartedly.

'It's all over, Penny. No harm done. He's going away and he won't be here any more. I don't suppose we'll ever see him again.' She stroked the thick hair back from the girl's dirty, tear-streaked face. 'Come along, darling, we must get into the house and up to your room. I don't think anybody will be about just now.'

Clare thought it was almost certain that Thelma would be lolling about the sitting-room with her romantic magazines and could easily be avoided. She just hoped that dratted child was well out of the way, too. Wiping Penny's face as clean as possible with her own apron, she led her quickly back to the house. Once inside Penny's pretty blue-and-white bedroom she drew a breath of relief.

'Have a bath, Penny, dear, and get to bed. I'll make excuses for you. A rest will do you good. Forget Louis and don't worry any more.' She helped the girl off with her ripped dress. 'It might mend all right, Penny.'

With a show of temper Penny snatched the dress back and rammed it down in a wastepaper basket. When she was in the bathroom, Clare pulled out the torn garment and carried it away. It was only an old cotton one, after all — it wouldn't be missed. She hoped the memory of its last wearing would disappear just as quickly as the ill-fated dress. Soon afterwards she took a warm milky drink and aspirin up to Penny and found her already in bed, staring wide-eyed up at the ceiling.

'Drink this, Penny, and then go to sleep. Forget all about this afternoon. It won't happen again. Terry will look after you. Think about Terry — go to see him tomorrow.'

Clare kept on talking softly while she tucked her in and stroked her forehead, and presently she saw the tenseness leave the girl's face. A few minutes later she stole quietly away.

'Where is Penny?' asked Joseph at tea-time, as Clare had fully expected he would.

'She has a headache. I've put her to bed for a while,' she said.

'A headache? That's not like Penny. Is she really ill?' he wanted to know anxiously.

'No, just out of sorts. She's been out in the sun too long, I think. It has been really hot today, you know.'

Martha looked at Clare dubiously. 'I'll go up and see her later.'

'Well, if you're sure she's all right.' Joseph took a bite then looked up again. 'Seems to be one of those devilish days. The sun must have turned Louis's head, too — he's walked out. Quitted the job. So, Gilbert, I'm expecting you to be around to do more work till I can get another farm-hand.'

Clare drew a deep breath of relief. The last of Louis, thank heaven!

'If you paid more you'd maybe get more help,' growled Gilbert.

'You're a fine one to talk. You'll get stuck into it tomorrow, Gilbert, or you know what you can do. *You* can clear out, too.'

'Hear him, Father? Ordering me around as usual.'

'It's only right,' said Timothy. 'You need a roof — Joe needs help. That's the only answer to it.'

Gilbert grunted some ill-tempered reply, and his wife frowned at him. 'When are we leaving here, Gilbert? You said you'd find work in a week or two. I'm sick of being out here in the wilds.'

Joseph looked at her scornfully. 'The sooner you get him away from here the better, Thelma. And I haven't noticed you doing much about the place, either. Let's see you clear this lot away and wash-up for a change.'

'It's not my fault Gilbert's on the rocks — I'm not here to wait on you lot — '

'Neither is Clare. She could walk out at a minute's notice if it suited her, and I wouldn't blame her for the extra work she has taken on out of friendship.'

'It won't hurt you, pet,' said Gilbert, sensing danger. 'You wouldn't be so bored if you did a few things.'

'Sit down, Clare,' said Joseph quickly, as Clare made a move to rise from the table. 'Let Thelma do her share. You've done too much for us all already — and get this child of yours to help, Thelma. She's old enough.'

'Serve you right, then, if you get broken dishes,' said Thelma peevishly, clattering plates together. 'Go and run the water in the basin, Sandra.'

Clare sighed, sitting there and feeling helpless, thinking of the broken eggs Sandra had cast aside. She looked around the disordered table. Timothy winked at her and she smiled. Beneath his rough exterior that old man had a streak of humour.

Clare knew Joseph wanted to give her assistance, but the atmosphere was unpleasant, and she would not feel easy till the Gilbert Canning family had dispersed to other parts of the house.

So she went upstairs to look at Penny. The girl was sleeping peacefully and the room was rosy in the light of the setting sun. Clare was turning away when she found Martha standing behind her. They went out together and when they were well away down the passage, Martha put a hand on the other's arm.

'Those scratches on Penny's face — '

Clare felt cornered. 'I think she fell in some brambles playing with the puppy — or something — '

'Oh, come on, Clare. There's more to it than that. Tell me, why has Louis suddenly cleared out.' As Clare still seemed confused, Martha said, 'It's to do with Penny, isn't it?'

'He was knocking her about, Martha. Trying to make love to her.' Clare gave a shaky laugh. 'I went for him with an old rake. I was going to tell Joseph if he didn't leave at once.'

'He'd have thrashed him nearly to death, at least. Good for you, Clare. But you wouldn't have hit him with the rake, would you?'

'Yes, I would! I was blazing mad — I saw red — ' Clare put a hand to her mouth, aghast at herself, shivering, remembering . . .

'I've always disliked him, too. Beneath all that handsome conceit lurks a devil. We're well rid of him, but I hope Joe can soon find a replacement.'

'What will I do if he notices Penny's face?'

'He won't. He's too busy to notice much. If he sees her around again he'll be satisfied.'

'Poor Penny! What with Sandra and Louis she hasn't been so happy lately.'

'It won't be for long now. Joe is getting more impatient as the days pass. It will rise to a pitch before long,' said Martha.

9

Some of Joseph's impatience broke out in the week following. Sandra came in from the yard howling. Her face was scarlet, her hair disarrayed and loose from its ribbon band.

'Whatever's the matter, pet?' asked her father, greatly astonished. His brazen little daughter was rarely in tears. Her mother came running from the sitting-room. Martha and Clare who had almost finished preparing the tea, stopped and stared.

'Uncle Joe beat me! He lifted me up and beat me!' Sandra threw herself against her father, sobbing.

Gilbert's face reddened. He got up and squared his shoulders as Joseph strode in. 'How dare you touch my child!' he stormed.

'If you gave her a few whackings yourself she'd perhaps behave herself.'

Joseph's face was furious. 'That little vixen left all the gates open and the animals were all off up the lane. And you needn't say she doesn't know — it was done deliberately. She knows the rules of the farm well enough by now.'

Martha dropped some plates to the table with a rattle. 'My God! Penny's Pride! If any harm comes to that pony I'll give her a hiding myself.'

'You'd no right to touch Sandra — ' said Gilbert, as Martha dashed out to the yard.

'If you don't like it and can't keep a check on her yourself, then you'd better go,' said Joseph icily. 'We'd be better off in every way without you lot here.'

'Well — ' Gilbert turned away, vanquished. 'As soon as I get a job — '

Sandra had stopped crying and looked interested with the argument she had caused. Clare guessed that her dignity was more hurt than her well-upholstered little body.

'As you haven't found that job yet you can come with me now and help to get the animals back,' said Joseph; 'and the byres want swilling out.'

'There's Dan — '

'He's mending a barn roof ready for the winter. Come on, Gilbert, get moving. The cattle won't have strayed far, but Tilly's missing — '

'Tilly?' Clare exclaimed. She picked up some sugar-lumps and was at the door instantly. She guessed only too well where Tilly would make for.

She went down the lane, calling the mare, searching as far as she could see. Presently she was climbing the moor beyond the farm meadows and there was Tilly, trotting contentedly towards Hilltops. As the horse disappeared into a dip she quickened her steps. She was almost at the farm-gates of Hilltops when Richard appeared, leading Tilly back by a halter he had thrown about her neck.

'This is yours, I believe,' he said, his eyes twinkling, not at all ill-humoured about it, as he would have been months ago. 'I think we ought to buy her and let her spend the rest of her days with her lover-boy.'

Clare laughed breathlessly. 'Yes, our crazy Tilly. I'm sorry, Richard,' and she went on to tell him what had happened.

'Well, we can't blame Tilly this time, can we? Come on, I'll walk her back with you. At least this has given me another chance to be with you.'

They strolled back over the dry, brittle grass. There had been little rain and the earth was hard-baked, the grasses snapping under their feet. The moors had a brackish, spent look. As they walked side-by-side, Richard leading the horse, he put his other arm over Clare's shoulders.

'We never went up to High Tor again, did we? Let's drive up there tomorrow, before the winter sets in.'

'Yes, I'd like to go again.'

'Walk down the lane tomorrow at our usual time. I'll be waiting for you with the car.'

It was raining next morning and Clare watched the leaden skies and straight hard rain with anxiety as she went about her cooking. Martha glanced out at it with satisfaction.

'This will do the garden good,' she said. 'Thank goodness the hay is all in, stacked high and dry.'

Clare went on whisking Yorkshire pudding mixture. Her day would be ruined if this went on. Not much point in going 'up to the top' in this. Yet before noon the rain had slackened and gradually ceased, and by the time she left the farm it was fine. No sun in sight but fine.

'What a morning!' she said, as she got into the car beside Richard. 'I was quite sure our date would be off.'

'Not so good even now for our view,' he said. 'We'll probably run into mist, but never mind.'

Water splashed high from puddles as they swept over the rough road, between hedges dripping with moisture. The road wound at treacherous angles, sometimes below high banks, tangled hedges and old mossy walls. Ever rising higher, leaving all habitation behind except an odd weathered barn or two. A waterfall tore down with its fresh flooding of rain into a steep gully. They drove into pockets of mist and out again.

'Perhaps we ought to turn back, Richard. We'll be getting lost in the mist.'

'I wouldn't mind, would you?' He looked down at her, his eyes warm and caressing.

At last they came to what seemed to be the highest point for miles around and Richard stopped the car. The mist had drifted away for the moment, shrouding some of the hills in the distance. Far below a river looked a narrow grey streak. The autumn shades of bronze, orange and yellow were here.

'It still looks beautiful even wet through,' said Clare happily.

'It's freshened it up, possibly.' He turned to her. 'I could stay here with you for hours, Clare. Miles away from everybody and no interruptions. I hope the mist comes back and surrounds us and we can't move.'

'Oh, Richard, not that. What an awful thought.'

'It's the only time I can really get you to myself.' As she was silent, he bent over her, his arm slipping round her shoulders. 'Clare, I'm madly in love with you. You know that, don't you?'

As she was still silent, fighting her own longings and fears, he lifted her face with his other hand under her chin, and pressed his lips firmly to hers. For a moment she relaxed, longing for Richard's love more than anything in the world, then she suddenly tried to draw away from his caresses.

'No, Richard — '

'But you care, don't you, Clare? I felt sure you did. I love you and want to marry you.'

'No, Richard,' she said again. 'We haven't known each other long. You know nothing at all about me.'

'I'm quite happy with you as you are, my darling. You'll marry me, won't you?

You love me enough, don't you? You *do* love me, Clare?' he repeated urgently.

She strove to deny this but, even though she felt she could not tell him the truth about the troubled past that always haunted her, neither could she tell him lies.

'Yes, I do love you, Richard, but I'm sorry — it's all quite impossible. I can't marry you.'

'Why ever not?' He laughed gaily. 'You're not already married, are you?'

'No, of course not.'

'Then nothing else matters.' He bent and kissed her once more, sure of himself.

'But it does. I can't let you go on loving me, Richard. I can't explain, but there are reasons — '

He thought a moment, his arms still clasped about her. 'I've rushed you, I suppose. Clare darling, if we wait a while, is there any hope for us — ?'

'Well, perhaps — ' she returned doubtfully. Oh, if only a time would come when her past could be wiped clean away and forgotten!

'Then I'll try to be patient and wait.'

'I really shouldn't see you again, Richard — that is, meeting you, going about with you.'

'Oh, nonsense. You must see me, Clare. I'll try to be patient, but I can't go on not seeing you. Come over just as usual, darling.'

'All right, but I've made no promises, you know. It's all so impossible for me. Some day — perhaps — I'll tell you all about it, but not now, not yet, Richard.'

'I'm quite happy as things are for the present. You care about me, so that's a good start.'

They sat a while at ease with each other, her head against his shoulder, wishing this peacefulness could last for ever. Wishing she could be frank with him without losing his love and respect.

'I think we'd better set off for home, after all,' he said, straightening up. 'The mist seems to be gathering again.' He grinned down at her. 'And I don't suppose it would be wise to get trapped up here for the night as things have turned out.'

'Yes, we'd better go,' said Clare soberly. 'I'm a bit nervous driving in mist, anyway.'

They drove slowly and carefully downwards from the high deserted moors, and back through the thickly misted dales. Clare told him about Louis going and Joseph being short-handed now.

After a thoughtful silence Richard said, 'I believe I can get Joseph help before long. If he doesn't mind young lads.'

'I don't suppose he would, so long as they work well.'

'Twins, just left school. They're down in the Midlands potato-picking at the moment. I'll see what they say when they get back.'

'I don't know — ' Clare hesitated, flushing. 'Richard, if Joseph knows you've sent them — '

'Don't worry, Clare. My name won't come into it. I'll make sure of that. The boys will arrange things for themselves.'

'Well, if he doesn't find anyone in the meantime . . . '

'I don't think he will,' said Richard. 'There aren't many farm-minded chaps around. They make for city lights, but these Melton boys love the country life. Aim to be farmers themselves some day.'

'They sound ideal. Thanks, Richard.' She looked at him with love in her eyes and he put his hand over hers.

As they reached Moorlands, Martha came up the yard leading Penny's Pride back to the stable. She looked somewhat astonished to see them, then came towards them. 'A bit raw for him to stay out, I think,' she said, her hand on the pony's neck.

Richard stroked the thriving, glossy black pony. 'He's a beauty, Miss Martha.' His eyes laughed at Clare. 'Dead image of his dad.'

'Mr. Layton — ' Martha started, then paused uncomfortably.

'Don't you worry about it, Miss

Martha. Your little mare has good taste after all — nothing but the best for her! Well, I'll get along now, Clare. Good evening to you both.'

He strode away and was soon lost in the drifting haze. 'He thinks a lot of you,' said Martha, as the sound of the car died away.

'I'm afraid he does, Martha.'

'Afraid?' Martha's voice held amazement. 'Don't let my old dad and Joe influence you.'

'I don't want things to get too serious — too involved. I'm all right as I am.'

'It's my guess he'll be a persistent young man.'

Clare did not answer. She had no desire to go into long explanations and evasions with Martha.

★　★　★

It was October before the Melton boys presented themselves at Moorlands, asking Joseph for work, and he was so glad to have help within his reach at

186

last that he was ready to accept them from the first. They were tall for their age, slim, wiry, both very fair — almost white. Fresh-looking, wearing tight jeans and plaid shirts. They kept up a continuous conversation between them.

'I'm Jimmy,' said one. 'And I'm Johnny,' said the other.

'And we heard there was a job here,' said Jimmy.

'But we always stay together, work together,' said the other.

'We'll do anything, though.'

'Because when we're older we want to have our own farm.'

'You look all right to me,' said Joseph quickly, as the young ones drew fresh breath. Behind him old Timothy, highly amused, chuckled. 'Start as soon as you like.'

'We'll start now,' they said together.

'Up the yard with you then,' said Joseph. 'I'll find you something to do.' He stared at the shining fair hair. 'You'll stay for mid-day dinners, I expect.'

'Sure, thank you, Mr. Canning,' they said together.

Life was easier for Joseph from that day. The boys were fine little workers, willing to do anything, intent on learning all they could. Whistling as they fetched and carried, digging, feeding and swilling. Nothing seemed beyond their power or below their interest.

'They're worth their weight in gold,' said Joseph. Then sadly, 'It's too good to last.'

'How are the boys shaping?' asked Richard, a week or so later, as he and Clare dismounted from their horses at their customary place.

'Everything in the garden's lovely,' laughed Clare. 'You've done wonders for Joseph.'

'They're an amazing couple, aren't they? But you can't help but like them. We had them for a while, you know, during the sheep-shearing. They did our regular jobs and left us free for the sheep.'

'They appreciate everything, too. They have a tremendous appetite, but then see how they work.'

'They were brought up by a rather old-fashioned aunt, but she was like a mother to them. She seems to have done something for them.'

'They have no time for Sandra, though she hangs around.' Clare laughed again. 'But then who has?'

'When is that lot going?' asked Richard.

'I've no idea, but I don't think it will be long before Joseph sends them packing. There's a lot of friction all the time.'

His arm was around her shoulder. He bent and kissed her cheek. 'Have you decided to marry me, yet?'

She gave a sudden start. 'Oh no, Richard. Don't hurry me. Give me time. I'm not so proud of my past, and I'd never marry you without telling you all about it.'

'I don't care about your past. It's now that matters. The past is all over and done with.' He gathered her to him and kissed her fervently. 'Clare darling, hurry up and say yes. I love you so much.'

'I don't want to start explaining yet, Richard. Leave it for a while longer, because the past does matter to me. I only wish I could wipe it all out and make a new beginning — with you.'

'All right, darling. I'll go on waiting, but I only want you to marry me and not start making confessions. I know you are a good girl, so any silly explanations will make no difference.'

'It's how I want it, Richard. How it must be.'

'Very well, my dear. I'll go on trying to wait patiently. While you love me I know there's hope.'

I ought to leave, she thought miserably as they sat in silence, her head resting against his shoulder as before. Why do I keep hanging on? It's not fair to Richard, and supposing Joseph ever found out? He would be angry and as hard as ever he was.

With the help of the twins Joseph had more time to himself and to notice how often Gilbert disappeared, shirking all he could upon the farm, and how little Thelma did. Seeing her lazing about and reading her magazines, complaining about the chilly sitting-room. There was rarely a fire in that quiet room facing south, they were too busy to sit about there. Clare, herself, liked the moors and the fresh air best when she was free, and at other times the solitude of her own room on the far side of the house.

Joseph's temper did not improve when he saw his brother having a gay time with some friends in a nearby town. He was bitterly angry when he saw how unkind Sandra was to Penny, when he caught her pulling faces and mimicking her, and he had hard work to hold back from shaking his niece. Penny wasted hours looking for things that Sandra had taken and hidden, and she found herself locked in a barn by the other girl once or twice.

At last one day Penny lost her calm forbearance, when she and Clare came across Sandra and an excitable Laddie chasing a young nervous horse around a field. The dog was yapping at its legs and Sandra was swishing at it with a branch.

'Sandra, what are you doing?' cried Clare, distressed. 'Laddie, come here at once!'

The dog veered at the well-known voice of one he adored and came shamefacedly towards her, tail drooping between his legs. The pony reared, snorting, then backed away. Penny threw herself at Sandra, slapping angrily at her, the two of them rolling soundlessly in the grass, till the younger girl started screaming.

Martha came running, Joseph at her heels. 'What on earth — ?' cried Martha.

'Sandra was chasing the horse, hitting at it — ' Clare had picked up the switch and held it out towards the others.

'Pablo was put in this field because he's so timid,' said Martha angrily. 'I was trying to get him to be friendly and trusting. A fine lot this will have helped.'

Clare was holding the quivering Laddie. Martha strove to calm and smooth down the sweating horse with a cloth she held, and Joseph hauled Sandra off the ground, out of Penny's fierce clutches.

'Get back into the house and stay with your mother!' he shouted, shaking her violently. 'We've had enough of you. I'll see your father when he gets back.'

Pushing the loose hair from her scarlet-cheeked face, the girl ran off. Joseph pulled a tearful Penny from the grass and held her against him comfortingly.

'You've had enough, Penny lass,' he said softly. 'Tomorrow we'll get rid of them.'

His daughter looked up and gave a wintry smile. 'And not before time, too,' said Martha, leading the quietened horse away to its stable.

10

They were all finishing tea when Gilbert's car rattled into the yard and a few minutes later he came in, looking highly pleased with himself.

'So there you are at last!' said Joseph without preamble. 'What are you looking so happy about?'

'I met some of my old pals — '

'Those I saw you with last week, I suppose.'

'Well, yes. I had a bet and I've won twenty pounds,' Gilbert said triumphantly, slapping a bundle of one pound notes on the table.

'So it's been a successful day,' said Joseph, ignoring the money, in a cold tone that should have warned his brother.

'I'd say so, wouldn't you?' Gilbert grinned at his moody-faced wife.

'Have you found any work today?'

demanded Joseph.

'No, of course not. There's nothing around here — '

'Perhaps not to your taste, but you haven't tried to find anything. So you can get back to where you came from and get work there. I want you out, Gilbert. You've been here weeks on end. I'm telling you now to pack and get out tomorrow.'

'Now, look here, Joseph — '

'You've done hardly anything to help. What you've done some days I could have done myself with an extra hour. And we can't stand that child of yours. She's a little devil.'

'You've no right to say that. You can't turn us out. We haven't the house now and what we got out of it the mortgage took most of it.'

'I've heard all this before. Go to Thelma's people. I know they offered to take you in at first. Let *them* have the pleasure of your company. You're going tomorrow — if I have to throw your belongings out myself.'

'This was my home. Father's master here — '

Timothy arose and went to his rocking-chair. 'Leave me out of it, Gilbert. You've had your chance, and you'll never make a farmer. Reckon you've outstayed your welcome.'

A spiteful look came into Gilbert's face. 'You can turn your own folk out but you give a home to a girl like that!' He pointed at Clare whose face turned suddenly pale. 'If we go she goes, too.'

'Don't talk such nonsense!' Joseph returned angrily. 'Leave Clare alone. We've known her for months and there's no one here better than Clare.'

'You have *not* known her. You know nothing about her. I thought I knew her face, that I'd seen her before some-where. I met your man Louis last week and he told me a thing or two. I let it slide but now you're going to know — hear about the criminal you're harbouring here.'

'How dare you talk like that!' Joseph was on his feet, advancing upon his brother as though he would strike him down. Thelma, Martha and Sandra watched wide-eyed, astounded into silence. Penny looked frightened, her hands tightly clasped.

'Ask her to deny it, then,' went on Gilbert scornfully. 'She's a jail-bird — a murderer. She's been in jail for murdering her old uncle. So what about that?'

Clare sprang to her feet, two red spots burning in her cheeks, her hands clenched on the table edge to support her trembling legs. 'I did *not* murder my uncle!' she cried.

'So you say, but who can prove you didn't?' jeered Gilbert.

There was a dead silence. Clare's bent face was now drained of all colour. Her brief happiness was at an end. It was all quite useless. The past had caught up with her.

'You're telling us nothing new,' came Timothy's voice quietly from the background. 'We knew all about it, but we took Clare on trust. We believe

Clare, so whatever you say makes no difference here. I'm simply sorry my own son should be so evil as to try to blacken the name of this young woman.'

Clare stared in surprise at the old man, blessing him for his timely support. She racked her brains, watching Gilbert's face with its sneering smile fading away, trying to think how she had slipped up. How had Louis found out? Surely she had destroyed everything that would give her away!

Joseph drew his large body up to its full height. 'Where did Louis get all this beastly information from?' he asked, as though he guessed Clare's frantic thoughts.

Gilbert shrugged. 'He'd searched around, he said, for anything to show who she was. Coming out of the unknown as she did. He was always suspicious. One day he came across an envelope addressed to a Miss Clara Durban — tucked in a far corner, somewhere in her car. He took it and the number of her car, and when he left here he went south and made enquiries. Simple, he said.'

Clare sighed. As simple as that! She recalled Louis's ugly look when she had last seen him. 'You'll pay for this . . . Somehow I'll make you pay for this!' he had thrown back at her.

'I didn't take much notice at the time, it paid me not to,' Gilbert was saying. 'But now — turning us out . . . '

'Yes. Well, as you now see we know all about it and believe in Clare, your story has lost its effect on us.' Joseph gave his father a look of gratitude. 'You've shown yourself up in your true colours. So get off to your rooms the three of you and get ready for leaving.'

Gilbert turned to his father, but the old man was packing his pipe, his face expressionless. Clare had moved around the table to his chair. Gilbert knew he was defeated. His last card was a failure. He went across to the inner door.

'Come on Thelma — Sandra,' he said, his voice flat and hopeless.

When the others were alone, Clare put her hand over Timothy's wrinkled one. There were tears on her cheek. 'Did you really know?' she whispered.

'Of course I knew, child. Soon after you came here.' His thin cheeks creased in a smile. 'I came by an old newspaper. There was a photo of you and all about it.'

'You said nothing — to anyone?'

'Why should I? I liked you, lass. I took you on trust as Joe did.'

She turned to Joseph. 'It's true I was arrested, Joseph, and was in prison some time for murdering my uncle, but there was not enough evidence to prove I did it. I swear, Joseph, I never did it — I've never hurt anyone.'

This time Joseph's hands closed over hers. 'Sometime you can tell me all about it, Clare, but not now. Of course we believe you, don't we, Martha?'

Martha coughed, choked, nodded her head. 'After all you've done for us, Clare, how could we help but believe? I would say we know you better than anyone.'

'I'll have to leave, though,' said Clare sadly. 'Louis will spread it everywhere — he hates me. He'll see that — the Laytons — everyone hears about it. Another hit at you, too. It won't be fair to you for me to stay.' She halted as Penny suddenly flung herself into her arms, silently crying.

'You're not leaving here because of this,' said Joseph firmly. 'Tell me, why does Louis hate you? Why did he go away so unexpectedly?'

Clare looked about her helplessly. Martha said crisply, 'He was worrying Penny. Making love to her — Clare forced him to clear out.'

'Forced him?'

Clare gasped. Martha would remember the rake, coupling it with her fierce anger and now the news of the mysterious death of her uncle. Yet the other woman said placidly, 'She was coming to tell you if he didn't leave at once.'

Joseph nodded, his face back in stern, set lines, thinking. Half an hour later they heard the farm's van backing out of the yard and knew Joseph was going off somewhere. Rather an unusual hour for him, unless perhaps he was going over to see Dora. Martha went to the door. 'Where are you going?' she called.

He came back from opening the wide yard gates. 'Tell Clare not to worry. I'll fix Louis. I'll find him if I stay out all night and I'll nearly break his neck for what he did to Penny and Clare. And I'll threaten him with libel if we ever hear another peep out of him.'

'Oh, Martha, he shouldn't go,' said Clare anxiously, as the van made for the outside lane. 'It's better for me to leave here.'

'Scoundrels like Louis deserve all that comes to them.' Martha turned and put her strong hands on each of Clare's shoulders. 'I know you could have lost your temper and would have bashed him with that rake, but I still don't believe you killed that old man.'

'Of course she didn't,' said Timothy. 'Is there any more tea in that pot, Martha? I've got a real thirst.'

'The tea's cold, but I know where there's a spot of something stronger.' Martha wagged a finger at him. 'You artful old fellow!'

'Well, someone has to have a bit o' sense around here.' He looked up at the ceiling at movements overhead. 'I'm right glad they're going, too. It's not like home with them around. That drink — make it sharp, Martha lass.'

Clare went often to the window, looking out at the deserted yard, unable to settle, waiting for Joseph to return. Martha was quietly stitching away at something, old Timothy and Penny had gone off to bed, and the others were still upstairs. Dark had fallen early after a dull, brooding sort of day. These Cannings were so good to her, trusting her in spite of it all, and Timothy was an old pet. They did not want her to go. But what of Richard? If she stayed on she would have to tell him — and how would he take it? It would be simpler to slip away, but, oh! what loneliness and misery again, more so with the sorrow of leaving her love behind. Ten o'clock came and went on the big, old-fashioned wall-clock.

'Come to bed, Clare,' said Martha, rising and straightening her work-basket. 'We needn't wait for Joe.'

'I wish he hadn't gone — '

'It was necessary to shut Louis's evil mouth.'

Clare started. 'Listen, surely that's the van. I think he's here, Martha.'

Shane rose leisurely from under the table and made for the door, tail waving with pleasure. Lights of the van swung into the yard, and presently Joseph came in. He bent to pat his dog but he looked strained, his lips pressed tight.

'You found him, Joe?' asked Martha.

'Certainly.' Joseph turned to Clare. 'You'll be all right now, Clare. I've made sure of that.' As she was about to speak, her lips feeling dry and stiff — 'Talk tomorrow if you wish, but now let's get to bed and forget it all for tonight.'

He went to the back kitchen and they heard water running as he bathed his face and drank. Clare bade them both good night and crept up to bed, but it was a long time before sleep came that night.

Gilbert Canning, Thelma and Sandra left early the next morning, a silent, disgruntled trio, the battered car jolting fussily out of the yard, then a wonderful peace seemed to descend upon the house. Clare was cleaning the sitting-room, picking up Thelma's discarded magazines, when Joseph came in. He shut the door behind him.

'I hope you're not worrying about yesterday, Clare. I can't say how sorry I am about Gilbert saying such things.'

She smiled faintly. 'It was such a relief when you and Mr. Timothy stood up for me — even though you have every cause to distrust me.'

'Far from it, Clare. We know you too well to listen to any scandal, and we know how much Gilbert can make of anything to suit himself.'

'What about Louis?'

'Louis knows where he stands. He'll only be fit for bed for a day or two, I'm afraid.' He moved over to the desk as though he had said all he meant to say.

'Joseph, I want to tell you — though you know most of it. I call myself Clare Bowers now, because Bowers is my middle name, after my grandmother. When my father died I went to live with his older brother, Uncle Ronald. I had no one else and he was glad to have me, always something of an invalid. He gradually got worse and, after I had been there a year or two, he had to spend his days in bed, with Mrs. Staines, his old faithful nurse, and me looking after him. It was a big house with a cook and daily helps, but there was plenty of money and he wanted for nothing — except good health. He was bitter about his helplessness, lying there like a useless doll, as he would say.'

Clare drew a deep breath. Joseph

waited, his solemn eyes on her face. She went on, 'He seemed worried I'd get tired of looking after him and go away. He used to grip my hand and beg me never to go. 'Stay with me, Clare,' he'd say. 'And I'll leave you everything I've got. I've made a Will. Nurse will be well looked after, but the rest will come to you. There's no one else.' He said it so often and Mrs. Staines must have heard sometimes — she'd come in, always jealous. She doted on him, been with him most of his life. He had to have tablets — dangerous things we'd been warned, and the bottle was kept in a safe place, out of the room.'

'Go on, Clare,' Joseph urged, as she halted again. 'Let's hear it all while we're about it.'

She sighed. 'Mrs. Staines was away at a relative's all that night, and I was left to take him his last milk drink. Next morning early he was found dead. Mrs. Staines went for the bottle of tablets and found it almost empty. She accused me at once, spread it to the doctors and everyone else. There was the inquest and, of course, Uncle Ronald had been poisoned with those tablets. What else could they do but arrest me? I couldn't prove my innocence. I was the only one there that night, I slept in an adjoining room in case he rang for me. I gave him his last drink and the glass had been taken away and washed.'

'But, good heavens, Clare — that woman could have done it herself. She came into quite a substantial sum, didn't she?'

'Yes, and the house, but she wasn't there that night, remember? She found him in the early morning, but he had died hours before that. I thought about it till I was sick. I was kept in prison and I thought it was the end. Then a barrister, a friend of my father's, fought for me. There was not enough proof — eventually I was released. But the damage was done and I could feel nobody believed I was innocent, Mrs. Staines saw to that. I had to get away — I had enough money to go anywhere, so I said I'd go abroad. I left my car miles away and said I'd sold it. I took a taxi to Dover, and from there I — disappeared. But I swear on anything you like, Joseph, that I didn't kill my uncle.' Her eyes met his, imploringly.

'I know you didn't,' he said at once. 'You were found 'not guilty' and that is enough for us. We believe in you, Clare.'

'I didn't go abroad — I felt too lonely and lost. It seemed too big a step. I picked up my car and came north. Scotland, I thought, then Tilly — '

'Tilly stopped you. Clare, listen to me. You can be happy here. We believe and like you. Your word is enough for us.'

'I can't tell you what my stay here has meant to me. You have been so kind. It's been like a new world.'

'Clare — ' he paused, walking to the desk and back, and she stared in surprise at his uncertain tone — 'I've thought about this for some time. Why don't you marry me? I'm fond of you

— I think we could make a good thing of it together.'

She flushed, taken unawares, rising from the chair she had sunk into in a state of exhaustion. Recalling that awful time had taken more out of her than she had expected.

'I'm sorry, Joseph, but I couldn't make a — a marriage of convenience. I'd have to be in love, and I'm sorry — '

'I'd like to start again, get married again. I've felt lonely too long, and as things are for you — '

'No, Joseph. I like you very much, but not for marriage.'

He drew himself up, his big frame looming over her. 'There's someone else, isn't there? You're in love with that young Layton fellow, is that it?'

She nodded. 'Yes, Joseph, but it's all quite impossible. I think I must go away at once now. It will be better for all concerned.'

'No, you're staying here, at least for a time. Forget what I said, it doesn't matter. We appear to be the only friends you have, so you need us. It's a pity about Richard Layton. As you know, we have no time to spare for any of them. Have you told him your story?'

'No.' She shook her head sadly. 'I've tried to several times but I dread the consequences. To see his face change, to see disgust, horror there — '

'Has he asked you to marry him?'

'Yes, but I've been unable — I've made no promises.'

'Look, Clare, tell him.' He slapped his hand hard on a chair back. 'If he believes you, still loves you in spite of it all, I'll apologise for all I've said about him. Tell him — let's see what stuff he is made of.'

She shook her head and moved over to the door. There she paused, met his stern gaze again. 'All right, I will. Next time I see him, I'll try to tell him.'

11

A week or two passed, yet Clare was still afraid of the future and kept out of Richard's way as long as she could. Then she met Jess in the village. 'Where have you been, Clare?' asked Jess. 'We haven't seen you for ages.'

'I'm kept busy,' said Clare lamely. 'The days slip past.'

'Everything all right at Moorlands?'

'Yes, of course. It seems peaceful now Joseph's brother and family have gone away.'

'That's Gilbert, isn't it?' Jess sniffed. 'A slip-shod mischief-maker. Joseph's no angel, but Gilbert's no match for him.'

'I couldn't agree more.'

'Well, Clare, Richard has missed you a lot.' Jess's eyes dwelt thoughtfully on the other's grave face. 'He says if he doesn't see you by tomorrow he's coming over to Moorlands to look for you.'

'Oh no, please tell him not to do that,' said Clare hastily. She wouldn't risk Richard turning up at the farm, disturbing Joseph and the old man. 'Tell him I'll meet him at the usual place.'

Jess searched her face. 'I thought you and Richard — you haven't quarrelled, have you?'

'Of course not.' Clare sighed. 'It's been difficult for me — something I can't explain just now, but believe me, Jess, I would never hurt Richard.'

'You know your own business best, but I just thought — knowing those Cannings, they could easily turn you against us.'

'Never in this world!' said Clare stoutly. 'You can be sure of that.'

'That's a relief. Richard's a good chap and he's gone simply crazy over you. I wouldn't like things to go wrong for him.'

And how wrong they might turn out to be, thought Clare, her hands clenched. Yet it had to be faced. 'Tell him tomorrow afternoon about the same time,' she said.

'Good. You don't know how relieved I am.'

A few minutes later Jess went back to where she had left her chestnut horse tied, and Clare watched her trot out of the village and up towards the moors, her back straight, hands loose on the reins. She never looked so well as when on horseback.

It was still in an uneasy frame of mind that Clare went to meet Richard the next day. Pulled both ways, she longed to see him again after keeping her distance for some time, yet dreaded having to tell him her terrible story. What would be the outcome of it? If she saw at once his face change to dislike and disgust, what then? For Penny's sake, at least, she hoped to remain in the district for a while yet, but how could she stand being so near to Hilltops if Richard changed towards her, loathing her? She couldn't blame him if he did. It would take a strong love to accept her as she was.

He was there waiting for her on the moors just above Hilltops. 'At last, Clare! Where have you been all this time?' He drew her closely into his arms and kissed her. 'I haven't given you cause to avoid me again, have I?'

'Of course not.' She pushed him gently away. 'Shadows from the past,' she murmured.

'What did you say?'

'Something turned up to unsettle me. I had to keep to myself for a time to think things out.'

'Well, I hope it brings new hope for me.' As she glanced at him with a shaky smile, he said, 'Do you want to ride? We'll go back for the horses, if you like.'

'No, I want to talk. Let's walk on, Richard.'

'Gilbert Canning and Co. have gone, haven't they?' he said, looking down at her curiously.

'Yes, and that was all rather unpleasant and disturbing, too.' Even if Gilbert hadn't spoken of it, it would have come out somehow, she thought, with a shiver.

'Cold?' he asked, his arm tucked in hers.

'No, just thoughts.'

They topped the rise and went down the rough beaten track on the other side. The sky was grey and lowering, bushes looking bare and straggling, and there was not another soul in sight. The world seemed to belong to them alone. She would never have a better opportunity for confidences.

'Richard, I told you I would explain everything some day, and now the time has come. What I have to tell you will shock you. But you will understand why I can't marry you and bring disgrace upon your family. I can only say I am innocent of all the lies they told about me.'

He took her in his arms again, holding her firmly against her weak protests. 'I love you, Clare. You don't have to tell me anything.' He bent and

216

pressed his lips hard to hers.

When she could speak, she struggled to keep her determination. It had to be today — she couldn't put it off any longer. 'I must tell you. You have to know, Richard. I can't delay it any longer — '

'But I do know, my darling.' He stroked the curly hair back from her forehead. 'I know all about it, what you are trying to tell me, and I love you more than ever if anything.'

'But how could you know?' She stared at him, aghast. Yet old Timothy had known. Was it possible that Richard, too, had seen that newspaper?

'I received an anonymous letter two weeks ago, and I took it for what it was worth. Wicked tittle-tattle.'

Angry colour rose to Clare's cheeks. 'Louis must have sent that letter. He told Gilbert and tried to make trouble for me at Moorlands!'

'Just as I expected. He is a vicious troublemaker — he did us a lot of harm on the sly. I was hoping we'd heard the last of him.'

'I'm sure we have now,' said Clare. 'Joseph beat him up afterwards, I believe.'

'That's the best news, yet.'

'I must tell you all about it, though, Richard. It's all quite true, you know — prison and all that, except that I was innocent. I didn't do it. I was fond of my uncle, and he was good to me in his way. I wouldn't have hurt him — '

'Clare darling, it makes no difference. I love you and we can be married now. The past is over — we'll never think of it again. You are safe here with me, and I know you and believe in you. Listen, darling' — as she tried to interrupt — 'I love you. You are all the world to me.'

Her face shone with relief and happiness. 'All the same, I want to tell you everything, then I'll feel I'm hiding nothing from you and we can start afresh. If only I could prove my innocence — '

'There's no need. I know enough and it means nothing.'

'I want to tell you. Let's walk on, Richard — it will seem easier.'

'Very well, if you must.'

He drew her arm through his and they walked slowly while she told the dismal story once again and she hoped for the last time. When she fell silent he halted and took her back into his arms, quite undisturbed, more comforting and affectionate than ever before. She knew then that all her fears were over. His love was deep and genuine, strong enough to conquer anything for her sake. They went down in the direction of the road and circled back to Hilltops. A great weight seemed to have been lifted from her shoulders. With a spring in her step, light-hearted, she walked beside him, a different being, and they talked and laughed of other things. The fears of yesterday were drifting away. Surely nothing could ever be as bad any more!

They had tea at Hilltops and Richard announced their engagement. All the Laytons appeared pleased. 'And about time, too,' said Jess bluntly. 'I thought you'd never make up your minds.'

'Well — ' Clare hesitated, flushing.

Richard put his arm about her shoulders. 'Clare was afraid I didn't know her well enough.'

'Oh, that!' Jess shrugged. 'I knew from the start you were made for each other.'

Richard laughed. 'Then I wish you had told us and saved us a lot of trouble.'

'How are Cannings going to take this?' asked his father.

Clare smiled. 'Richard is not their choice for me, naturally, but they won't be surprised. They've had an idea of the way the wind was blowing.'

'If they take it badly she will have to leave at once and come here,' said Richard.

'It would be nice if I could bring you two families together,' said Clare.

'Not much hope of that,' muttered Jess. 'I doubt whether fire or flood would bring us together.'

Richard accompanied her home as far as the boundary of Cannings' property. 'No more worries, delays or anything else,' he said, as they said goodbye. 'We'll be married in a few months, and by then I hope to have a little cottage modernised for us. I've been negotiating for it for some time.'

'You never told me,' she said, looking up from the shelter of his arms.

'Well, you never said you'd marry me, did you?' His eyes twinkled down at her mischievously. 'Though I thought you would in the end.'

'Did you indeed! Where is the cottage?' she asked eagerly.

'It was supposed to be a secret, but perhaps it would be as well for you to inspect it first. The other side of Lambreck, quarter of a mile from the village.'

'I know I'll like it, Richard,' she said excitedly, cheeks flushed. 'But I'd love to see it all the same.'

'And so you shall next time we meet. I never thought — you'll have to see it for curtains and fancy trimmings, won't you?'

Her own little cottage! A little corner to settle down in away from all the past sneers and suspicions at last! She walked back over the fields later, dreaming of Richard and their future together. The sky was darkening and the moors had never looked so lovely to her, rusty-coloured in the last red rays of the sun. She sighed blissfully. It was the end of a wonderful day.

When the Cannings heard about Clare's engagement to Richard Layton they took it in different ways. Penny looked delighted because it meant that her dear friend would not be going far away, after all. Martha wished her well, but could not hide her dismay at the prospect of being tied to the house and kitchen so much more again. Joseph took the news quietly but hoped she would be happy.

'I hope you've chosen right.' His eyes met hers steadily. 'But I think we've proved something, don't you? I suppose you did as I said?'

'Told him, yes,' answered Clare confidently. 'He already knew and just tossed it aside. He believes me. He trusts me.'

'Then he's made of better stuff than I thought.'

Timothy put his spoke in with his usual bluntness. 'Trust those Laytons to make off with you. I might have known they would — always want what we've got. If they don't treat you right, you come right back here, my girl.'

Clare laughed, knowing old Timothy would miss her as much as anybody. 'All right, I will. You can be sure of that.'

12

A week or so later Clare was tidying up the kitchen before following the others up to bed, when she was attracted by a red glow somewhere in the background, in the stable-yard. It deepened and flickered as she gazed and suddenly she sprang into action. Fire! It couldn't be anything else. She tore open the hall door and chased up the stairs, shouting for Joseph.

'Come quickly, Joseph. Fire! There's a fire in the yard!'

He was only half-undressed. Dragging on his jacket he rushed out of his room, and immediately afterwards Martha came down the passage pulling slacks over her pyjamas.

'Fire? Did you say fire?' Joseph gasped. His face told the rest, plainer than any words . . . 'Oh, not again!' it declaimed with horrible memories.

'It's up by the stables, I think,' cried Clare, scrambling down the stairs after him.

'Oh, my God, the horses!' moaned Martha, hot on their heels.

'Someone get the fire brigade if you can,' called Joseph. 'Maybe too late, but still — '

As they ran towards the stables they could smell burning and acrid smoke caught at their throats. The dogs were barking and worried, chasing madly up and down. Joseph fastened a hose to a tap in the yard, and Martha rushed past with buckets slopping over with water.

'I'll phone from Hilltops,' said Clare, hurrying to get her car.

Everything so old-fashioned and inadequate! she thought. A roaring blaze was already eating away at the big barn of foodstuffs, and flames flicking over to the nearest stable. Horses were already neighing with fright, sensing danger. Never had she driven so fast, recklessly swishing and bumping round the uneven narrow lane to the bottom road, and a minute later swinging to the right and up towards Hilltops. She slammed her brakes on as a car suddenly plunged out of the farm-gates then jerked to a stop. Richard jumped out and came towards her.

'I was coming over — ' he began.

'There's fire in a barn, Richard,' she panted. 'Near the stables. Please phone for the fire brigade. Please hurry!'

'Wait there. I won't be a minute. Turn your car around.' He rushed into the house and was back almost immediately. 'Come on, let's go,' he said. 'We'll be needed.'

As he got into Clare's car, Jess snapped open the rear door and sprang inside. 'We saw the red light and wondered if we ought to come over,' she said, hanging on to the front seat as the car swerved and jolted back towards Moorlands.

'It's time Joseph took more precautions,' said Richard. 'Two fires in about five years. No phone or fire appliances.'

'This will shake some sense into him

perhaps,' said Clare.

'Not before time,' added Jess coldly. 'If he gave more thought to necessities instead of throwing mud at his neighbours . . . '

Clare was silent, urging the car desperately in the direction of Moorlands, in no mood for calling the Cannings. They were dogged by ill-fortune. It was enough to embitter anyone's mind. As they tore into the farmyard, they found old Timothy and Joseph both fighting madly against the spreading flames with hose and buckets. The barn was an inferno, it would be an entire loss, and the first stable was alight and the others clouded with thick smoke. Jess had set Tilly and the young Penny's Pride free, and was now striving to get Pablo out, the timid horse that was rearing and kicking desperately.

'Grab Tilly, Clare, if you can,' said Joseph urgently, his blackened, tense face turned to her for a moment. 'She might bolt.'

Clare caught up a halter from a post and dashed after the two horses. Luckily Tilly came to her, knowing her voice and needing comfort, and she threw the rope about the animal's neck and led her to the nearest field. To her relief the young pony came closely behind them, as though still instinctively following his mother, and Clare shut the gate behind them, taking the rope and hurrying back to the yard. The crowd about the blaze seemed to have grown. Other farmers had rushed over to help, seeing the glare against the night sky, and more men from Hilltops. The small fire engine was dashing up. Richard was helping Martha to drag the petrified Pablo out and away to some secure corner, while Jess tried to get through the dense smoke into the larger stable where several horses were fastened in stalls, screaming with terror. Clare halted, wondering helplessly what she could do, the intense heat of the fire burning her face, and presently she became aware of something different, something odd, beyond the urgent activity of the crowd. Someone screaming wildly, screams that arose above those of the animals. Turning in astonishment she made out the figure of Penny, a thick coat thrown over her night clothes, her red-gold hair lifting in the slight breeze, and she was crying out *aloud* — at the top of her voice.

'Fire, Daddy! Fire! The fire!' repeating the word as though she would never stop, living again through her terrible nightmare of five years ago.

'Joseph!' cried Clare, clutching at his arm. 'Penny's here? Look at her! She's got her voice back!'

He glanced back at the terrified figure of his daughter, the flames lighting up her rich hair and pale face, her mouth working, crying out to him about the fire and other incoherent words.

'Oh, my God!' he uttered anxiously. 'Look after her, Clare. Try to comfort the poor child.'

Clare struggled back through puddles

of water and over hose-pipes and other objects that had been tossed out of harm's way, and at last reached Penny's side. At first the girl did not seem to know her, her eyes on the raging flames, trying to push her away. Then as Clare held on to her, folding her in her arms, she turned to her, whimpering.

'You can talk again, Penny!' exclaimed Clare. 'Isn't it wonderful? Oh, my darling, fright has brought your speech back.'

'The horses — ' said Penny breathlessly. 'Someone is in there — they'll get hurt.'

She was getting her memories of the previous fire mingled with this one it seemed, as words strange to Clare poured out, as though now she could speak she would never stop.

'It's all right, Penny. No one will get hurt. Don't be frightened, my dear,' murmured Clare.

She tried to coax the girl back to the house, but she would not move till she knew everyone and all the animals were safe. Clare wondered uneasily where

Richard was. With a wet cloth round his head he had dived through the smoke and was struggling to release the restless horses. Jess and Martha did their best to help, unhappy about their beloved animals, until Martha almost collapsed, overcome with the smoke and had to be taken away.

Words kept spilling miserably from Penny's unlocked lips. 'The horses — Tilly — '

'Tilly and her son are in a field, Penny,' soothed Clare, as they huddled together for warmth and comfort on the fringe of the crowd. 'Nearly all the horses are out now — they will all be safe soon — ' she broke off with a gasp as a burning beam fell, tossing out flakes of fire. 'Oh, Richard!' she moaned to herself.

He was in there somewhere amongst the falling debris and thick smoke.

The firemen were playing their hoses on the stables to prevent the fire spreading further. Tilly's stable and the big food barn were just about gutted, but the flames were diminishing. Richard had thrown blankets over the last horses and had been leading them to the door for his brother Stephen to take away out of danger, well away from the heat and flames.

'The horses are all out!' suddenly cried Timothy, his voice more than usual quavery with emotion.

'And they're getting the fire under control, thank God!' said Joseph with a deep sigh, as flickers of flame rose and fell at the extreme edge and hissing steam floated about them from the sizzling remains. Then as Penny came running to him, flinging herself into his arms, murmuring words, he said, 'My dear little Penny! Perhaps this has all been worth it after all.'

'Where is Richard?' almost sobbed Clare, then she shuddered as he appeared in the doorway again, a dishevelled, blackened figure, assisting out his sister.

'The falling beam caught her shoulder,' he said. 'I think her arm is broken and somewhat scorched. Can I have your car, Clare? I'll run her over to the hospital.'

'I'll be all right,' said Jess staunchly, yet looking faint with pain and far from her usual breezy self.

'You're going to see the doc, Jess, and at once,' said Richard. 'I'll be back, Clare.'

'So will I,' said Jess.

Yet when Richard returned soon afterwards he was alone. 'They're keeping her in for a day or so,' he told them. 'One or two burns they are anxious about, and of course the arm is broken.'

'I'm very sorry about that. All our fault again,' said Joseph miserably.

He and Clare were watching the firemen playing the hoses on the centre of the fire, still fighting the persistent flames where the barn had once stood. There seemed little more they could do themselves now they had the animals out of danger. Martha had taken Penny back to the house, and the Layton fellows were up by the van in which they had arrived, waiting for Richard to join them.

Joseph stuck out his hand. 'A bit late — but I'm truly grateful for what you've all done tonight, Layton. We don't deserve it after all the bitterness.'

'We couldn't just stand by,' Richard said. 'How do you suppose the fire started? No lanterns or anything like that around.'

'The firemen suspect paraffin and there was a tin lying just inside. But I know for a fact there was never anything inflammable about here.'

'Then it's been done deliberately.'

'It must have been — and I have a good idea who did it,' returned Joseph angrily. 'The work of a devil. That bastard who worked here, Louis. I gave him a good hiding for molesting Penny and Clare and this is his revenge.'

Richard nodded. 'I've been thinking for some time that he was the cause of a lot of trouble between us. Heaven knows why, but he's a real trouble-maker. For some reason it suited his purpose to keep us at logger-heads.'

'Time heals they say.' Joseph sighed. 'I was beginning to see things in a better light — then this happens. Yet I wonder — the shock has loosened Penny's tongue, did you know? She's talking.'

'That's tremendous news. I'm glad, Joseph,' said Richard warmly. 'She's a lovely girl.'

Joseph's face brightened. 'After all, Penny matters most. We can always build another barn. It could have been a lot worse.'

'That's true. You've been an unlucky family. If we can help at all — with anything . . . ' Richard hesitated, then went on, 'Don't be afraid to ask.'

Joseph nodded seriously. 'Thanks. I've learnt my lesson, the way you and your sister risked your lives tonight.'

'Well, you know Jess — it would break her heart to see an animal injured, especially horses. She will think it all worthwhile.'

'I hope she will soon be better. It's a rotten shame, I feel terrible about it.'

'By the way,' said Richard, 'she said, if you haven't room to house all the horses, we have a stable or two to spare till you build again, and we will help you with the feeding.'

'We could find room in the other barn for one or two,' said Clare. 'And we could fix Tilly and her pony up in the old storage barn at the end. If we pushed the spades and things to the back and put straw down.'

'Yes,' agreed Joseph. 'Luckily there are still some places still untouched. Pablo, the jumpy one, had better go into the small stable. About three horses will be left out, I think. If you wouldn't mind — er — Richard . . . There's frost in the air. Martha won't want them left outside.'

'Stephen and I will take them over. Now Clare and I had better get that far barn ready while you bring the horses in and sort them out. Keep them well away from this end or they'll never settle.'

'I'll help you, Joe,' came Martha's voice from the shadows behind. 'I'm all right now. Just feel as though I've swallowed a bucketful of soot.'

'What about Penny?' asked Joseph.

'I've put her to bed and given her a sedative. She seemed somewhat hysterical. But isn't it wonderful, after we'd given up all hope? It seems like a miracle.'

'I'll get the doctor to see her tomorrow to be on the safe side.'

'He said it might be only temporary paralysis, but five years — '

'It was the sudden shock, I suppose, as though it was all happening again, just the same. Must have released her in some way.'

'I've put Father to bed, too, with a hot water-bottle. This night air and exercise won't have done him much good.'

'Keep him in bed tomorrow.'

Martha gave a strained laugh. 'You

keep him there if you can.' She looked about her at the patient firemen and at the few other men who had stayed to help. The crowd had dwindled seeing that all danger was over at last, making their weary way back to their own homes and bed. 'Don't let anybody else leave yet, Joe. I'm bringing some tea and eats up in a minute.'

Inside the old barn where Louis had attacked Penny, Richard drew Clare into his arms and held her a moment. It was all so peaceful and comforting away from the terror of the last hours.

'I won't kiss you,' he said. 'I feel filthy.' Conscious of his grimy face and clothes and scorched hair.

'Oh, Richard,' she sighed. 'After we were so happy — if anything had happened to you I'd have gone mad.'

'Don't think about it, darling. The worst is over and it has its lighter side. It seems to have ended our age-long feud and given Penny her voice back. That's marvellous, isn't it?'

'Yes, as Martha says, like a miracle.

238

Drastic treatment. But poor Jess — '

'She'll soon pick up, don't worry. She's a strong lass.'

'I'll go over to see how she is tomorrow. Now we'd better hurry and get this place fixed, Richard. They'll be bringing the horses in before we're anywhere near ready for them.'

'I'll be down the road tomorrow if you'll pick me up,' said Richard, rolling a spare wooden wheel to the dark end of the building. 'Visiting hours are three to four.'

When Richard and Clare returned to the yard they found Martha dispensing hot tea and scones to everybody. She had stoked up the fire for hot water, and about five o'clock in the morning, when everything was safe enough and the firemen had gone, she, Joseph and Clare had a quick wash down and tumbled into bed. Too exhausted to lie fretting about the disaster and the unpleasant work facing them tomorrow. A quick look at Penny assured them that she was now resting peacefully, a faint smile on her lips.

Before breakfast they all, except Timothy and Penny who were still blissfully sleeping, went out to look at the blackened ruins. Smoke still drifted up from the hot charred wood and rubbish. They found Johnny and Jimmy looking in dismay at the ugly spectacle, and Dan came out of the nearest scorched stable after a sad inspection. The three of them had been asleep in bed at the time down in the village, so were shocked to find such a disrupted scene upon their arrival that morning. The boys' misery seemed tinged with disappointment that they had missed so much of the performance.

'Don't touch any of that yet,' said Joseph, as Johnny poked a stick into the smoking debris. 'It burnt for hours and it's still very hot, and the police will soon be here, so nothing must be disturbed.'

'How did it happen?' asked Dan. 'I never thought this would happen again.' His anxious eyes studied Joseph's face, remembering the horror of five years ago, and wondering how the other had taken it.

'Someone fired it, Dan,' said Joseph acidly; 'and I'll give you one guess who.'

Dan nodded. 'Aye, reckon I can guess who, the conceited bastard.'

'And with no help from the Laytons this time, either. In fact, Hilltops people were here and risked their lives for us, saving the horses. So we'll have no word against them in future.'

Dan did not trouble to remind him that he for one had never said a word against their neighbours. He turned to the boys. 'Come on, lads, it's getting late. We'd better get on with what work we can do.'

'There are some horses over at Hilltops till we get straightened out,' Joseph told him. 'And they are sending over some oats and corn some time today.'

About an hour later Terry arrived on his bicycle, looking hot and worried. He gasped at the sight of the ruined buildings, little puffs of smoke still spiralling out of what had been the main barn. Sergeant Allen from the village was turning over the rubble with one or two of his colleagues. He shook his head sadly as he saw Terry.

'There's a right mess here, isn't there? Seems to have been a bit of nasty work by someone.'

Terry struck his fist into his other hand. 'I never knew. I ought to have been here to help. When did it happen?'

'Started up around ten o'clock by what they say.'

'And I was in bed dead to the world, didn't know a thing about it. I hope — was anyone hurt?' asked Terry anxiously, thinking of dim tales he had heard of the previous fire.

'Nothing serious. I believe Miss Layton has a broken arm but they'll tell you all about that,' said the Sergeant, nodding towards the house.

Clare saw Terry coming across the yard and waited at the door for him.

'Hello, Terry. We've been having an awful time.'

'I'm sorry I didn't hear about it till this morning — just a while ago. I ought to have been here to help you all. Is Penny all right? It must have been terrible for her and her father, all this happening again.'

'Come in and have a cup of tea. There's still plenty in the pot. We're all seedy this morning, having breakfast at all times.'

He looked around the kitchen hopefully. 'Isn't Penny up yet?'

'It was a bad shock for her, of course,' said Clare carefully. 'We are keeping her in bed and the doctor will be coming to see her.'

Terry put his cup down. 'In bed — the doctor? What's it done to her? Let me see her — let me see for myself.'

'There's no need to worry, Terry — ' Clare halted as Martha came to the doorway from the back kitchen.

'No, don't worry, Terry. It's good news, but I think we ought to tell you

243

before you see Penny. We don't want her to get excited. You see, she seemed to go back to the first fire, living it all over again, and she was crying out — loud. *Loud*, Terry, do you understand? She's talking again!' Martha's eyes shone, and she twisted the cloth she held in her enthusiasm.

Terry stared, unable to believe his own ears. 'Talking?' he gasped. 'Penny is talking at last?'

'Yes, isn't it splendid!' Clare and Martha told him all about the night before. He sat down and gulped the tea remaining in his cup.

'Can't I see her — just for a minute?' he begged, as they came to a stop.

They looked at each other, considering, then Martha said, 'Well, only for a minute. The doctor always said if there was any sign of her voice returning we must take it slowly, let her get back to it gradually, and to let him know at once. It was a dreadful shock, too, don't forget, so we *must* keep visitors away.'

'I won't let her talk, Miss Martha.

Just to say how glad I am.'

They couldn't disappoint him, Clare's look told Martha. It was something of a red-letter day for him.

'Very well, but only a minute, mind. Take him up, Clare.'

Clare peeped into Penny's bedroom. The girl was lying on her back, staring out at the pale autumn sky with its fluffy white clouds, smiling at the little sparrow chirping busily on the window-sill.

'Here's Terry to see you, Penny.'

She turned, smiling radiantly as he went towards her, her blue eyes deep and glowing. 'I've orders not to stay,' he said softly. 'Only a peep at you.'

'Hello, Terry,' she said huskily.

He bent and kissed her, pushing his fingers up through her long thick hair. 'It's tremendous news, Penny love. I'm so glad for you.'

'Won't it be nice — now we can talk — to each other?' she said hesitantly. 'No more nodding — and writing notes.'

'Hush, love, you have to rest. I must go. I'm late for work as it is. We were draining that low field of Earnshaw's yesterday. It flooded the last rain and never gets away.' He bent and kissed her again. 'I'll be over some time tomorrow, Penny.'

'I wish they'd let me get up.'

'See what the doctor says. 'Bye, Penny love.'

He walked buoyantly downstairs and back to the kitchen. 'I still can't believe it. It seems too good to be true,' he said.

'It should make so much difference,' said Clare. 'She won't be so nervous or afraid of mixing with other people any more.'

'It's marvellous — absolutely simply marvellous!' Terry went across the yard, swinging his cap into the air jubilantly and catching it as it came down, walking quickly and gaily. The happiest man on the moors.

13

After speaking to the police Joseph had gone off somewhere in a police car that morning. He returned an hour or so later and stamped into the kitchen, his face red with fury.

'Where on earth have you been?' exclaimed Martha. 'We've had our hands full this morning, what with the police and other folks getting under our feet.'

'We've been trying to track Louis down,' said Joseph, taking a hunk of bread from the littered table and buttering it lavishly. 'But he's gone — scarpered — as we might have guessed.' He bit into the bread with strong, big teeth. 'Left his last lodgings yesterday — early evening. No one knows where he's gone or seen him since then. It's up to the police to find him now.'

'He won't come near here any more,' said Martha.

'That he won't. He's struck his blow at us.' He finished the bread and went to the back kitchen to swill water over his face and hands. 'I feel I'll never be rid again of all that smoke and dirt. How are the horses?'

'Pablo's jittery as you might expect,' said Martha. 'I don't know what I'll do with that pony. Perhaps Jess Layton can advise something.'

Joseph looked at her sharply, then held back the retort that rose to his lips. After all, they had agreed to forget past grievances with Richard Layton only a few hours ago. 'How are the others? Tilly?'

'Some of them are a bit uneasy yet, of course, but nothing to worry about. Tilly and her son are nuzzling each other and seem to like their dusty old barn better than the stables.'

Clare laughed. 'That Tilly is a real character. Life would be dull without her.'

At midday yet another visitor called at Moorlands. The boys, Joseph and Dan were drifting up towards the yard to be on hand for dinner to be announced, when Dora Walters rode in on her bicycle. She left her machine against a wall and crossed to where Joseph was wheeling big churns into the dairy.

'What a terrible thing to happen again, Joseph,' she said softly. 'You have the filthiest luck.'

'So it seems, but I suppose we'll get over it as before.'

'I've only just heard. I was up in Randgate last night to see a sick aunt. She wanted me to stay till my cousin arrived to look after her.'

'I see.' He looked at her thoughtfully. She looked a comely figure in her navy suit, her cheeks rosy with the keen air and tendrils of soft dark hair fluttering out from the light-blue headscarf. 'Now you are here you might as well stay for dinner,' he said.

'Oh, I don't know whether Martha

would like that — '

'There's always room at our table for more — and there'll be plenty, Clare sees to that. So no reason for Martha to object.'

'All right, I'd like to stay. I'll give you a hand with these small cans.' She turned and ran hot water into one of the quart cans.

'You'll mess yourself up.'

'That I won't!' She snatched a big apron off a hook and tied it on. 'I'm not that stupid.' A moment later she looked at him, her face anxious. 'Joseph, what about Penny? You've never mentioned her. It hasn't harmed her, has it?'

'Harmed her?' He chortled unexpectedly. 'It's given her a voice once more. She's talking at last!'

'Oh, Joseph, how wonderful!' Dora's face was overjoyed. She took a step forward then halted, her hands dropping to her side. She had almost hugged him in her delight, knowing this would make Joseph a more human, reasonable man now.

'My greatest wish granted, Dora,' he said gravely. After a few minutes silence as she returned to her task, he said, 'We've shaken hands with the Laytons. If it hadn't been for them we might have had great losses last night.'

'They are good people at heart, Joseph. I could never understand why you kept up that silly quarrelling.'

'*Why?*' he echoed coolly.

'What happened wasn't their fault. We can't be responsible for a cousin's failings.'

'No, I suppose not and — I would never admit it — but Ellen was as bad as that fellow was.' He slammed a churn down noisily. 'I've not been myself for some time, Dora. Seeing Penny as she was kept it all fresh in my mind, I suppose, and by what Richard Layton said, Louis must have caused a lot of mischief between us.'

'Whatever it was I hope your bad luck is at an end. You've certainly had your share.'

'Clare has been a great help. Penny adores her.'

'Yes, she is a nice girl,' Dora said quietly, suddenly thrusting her hands down into the soapy water.

'Did you know — she and young Layton are going to be married?'

Her face changed, shining with frank relief. 'That's grand news, too. He'll make her a good husband.'

'You think so?' — dryly.

'Oh, come, Joseph, you said you'd made your peace with the Laytons. What makes you have such a poor opinion of Richard?'

'Well, we'll see,' he said stubbornly. 'For Clare's sake I hope you're right.'

Footsteps came across the yard and Clare herself stood in the doorway. 'Come along, Joseph, dinner. Oh, hello, Dora! You've found us in a bit of a mess, haven't you?'

'I came over as soon as I knew, thought I might help in some way. If there's anything I can do . . . '

'Lay another place, will you, Clare?'

said Joseph. 'Dora's stopping for dinner.'

'Oh, good. A bit of company will cheer us up. If you can get a word in edgeways with those twins.'

'Has the doctor been? What did he say?' asked Joseph.

'He was here half an hour ago. We're doing right to keep her quiet. Another two days in bed at least, and to get her back to talking gradually — not to overstrain. He wants to avoid a relapse.'

'He thinks she will be all right now?' he asked worriedly.

The two women looked at each other. Penny's recovery meant new life to Joseph. It would be a load off his mind if the girl was quite herself once more. 'If we take care he doesn't see why not, Joseph,' Clare said steadily.

As they went across to the kitchen, Dora said, 'I've just heard about you and Richard. I'm very pleased, Clare.'

Clare smiled, her eyes mischievous, teasing Dora, knowing how really pleased she must be, the way being left open for herself at Moorlands. 'It's been pending for some time, but I couldn't make up my mind.'

'There you are, you see,' said Joseph, unusually amiable. 'Even Clare didn't know whether to trust the Laytons or not.'

'Oh, go on with you!' said Dora breezily.

She went to the kitchen to help with the serving, and Clare told her something of the fire. 'I'm going to see Jess this afternoon in hospital. She broke her arm helping with the horses — a beam fell on her.'

'Trust Joseph not to mention that, but I don't think it was intentional. His mind is full of Penny and other things.'

Clare laughed. 'I don't know just how much the Laytons will have to do to get his grudging praise.'

Except for the absence of Penny, dinner was pleasant enough, all of them shutting away the thoughts of the destroyed parts of the farm and the nerve-shattering night, for that short time. The police had gone and there was a certain sort of peace up in the stable-yard. The boys were a little subdued by the presence of a visitor.

Timothy watched Dora furtively, a gloating in his little sharp eyes. At last his thoughts getting the better of him, he said: 'It's kind of nice having plenty of women about the place again. Feels more home-like.'

'Just because they spoil you. So none of your old wiles, Father,' said Joseph, but he did not look annoyed as he might have done a week or two back.

'You didn't say that much when Thelma was here,' said Martha.

'You call that idle, skinny stick a woman? Don't know what Gilbert sees in her.'

'Cut it out, Father,' said Joseph. 'Gilbert's gone. It's none of our business.'

'Aye, you're right. Martha shouldn't have brought that up.'

'Have some more pie, Father, and shut up,' said Martha good-temperedly, cutting a slice and pushing it towards him.

'It'll be a pity when Clare goes to get wed,' persisted the old man. 'This pie fair melts in the mouth.'

'We'll find someone, Father,' said Joseph. 'Martha is too valuable with the farm work. We'll get someone for the house.'

'Anyway, she's not going yet — if she does go — knowing those Laytons.'

Joseph was about to rebuke him when Clare shook her head, preventing him, and silence fell for a few moments.

'I'll always help you out if you don't get fixed up with anyone, Joseph,' put in Dora, unable to hide her eagerness. 'Mother taught me to cook well.'

He looked up at her solemnly. 'I might take you up on that, Dora.'

'After all, we've been friends a long time. I'm free whenever you want me.'

Clare looked around at the Cannings, hiding her amusement. While Dora looked rosy and triumphant as though what she desired most lay ready to fall into her lap, Martha, too, had a satisfied look. Hadn't she just heard that her brother had no intention of taking her away from the farmyards and the animals? Timothy had a wide grin on his wrinkled brown face. Argumentative old terror that he so often was, he had a knack of seeing further than any of them and manoeuvring them into the position he wanted.

As Clare backed her car out to go over to the hospital that afternoon, Martha came running after her, pulling a coat over her slacks and jumper.

'Take me with you, Clare. I ought to see Jess after we've been so beastly, and after what she did.' She looked at the other uncertainly, feeling embarrassed by this change of attitude.

'Of course. Jess will be glad to see you.' Clare smiled. Martha and Joseph had led such a hard, friendless life for so long it was difficult for them to unbend and hold out a kindly hand.

They found Jess much better than they had expected, her arm in splints and a sling and almost her old forceful self again, threatening to walk out without leave if they didn't send her home soon. True to her word she was soon back at Hilltops, making light of her injuries, and before long rode over to the other farm to see how things were getting along there, her arm still firmly supported. Besides the food for the animals that Richard and his brother brought over they helped in many ways after that, repairing the partly burnt stables and helping to rush up the walls of a new barn before the winter set in properly.

Penny was by the newly boarded and cleaned stable, brushing down Tilly till the mare looked almost as shiny and coppery as her own mane of hair. She smiled radiantly at Jess. Her voice came, clear and sweet. 'Good afternoon, Miss Layton.'

'It's good to hear you speak after all this time, Penny. I'm very happy about it.'

Penny chuckled. 'You can guess I am,

too. I felt so stupid — '

'We never thought you stupid, Penny, did we, Jess?' said Clare, joining them. 'Never think that.'

'Will you have a look at Pablo for me?' Martha asked Jess. 'I'm afraid he'll never be much use. He jibes at the slightest noise.'

She led Jess to where the nervous horse watched them from a half-open stable door. 'I daren't let him out these days. It takes so long for me to coax him back.'

Pablo moved away as they drew near, the whites of his eyes showing. 'Come, Pablo, old man, what's the matter then?' said Jess softly. She unlatched the bottom half of the door.

'He'll rear, Jess,' said Martha anxiously. 'He doesn't know you.'

'He'll soon know me. Go and ask Richard to come here, will you?'

Martha hurried across to where the men were working and rushed back with Jess's younger brother. Jess was standing quietly up against the door, while Pablo snorted and pawed the ground. She was talking to him soothingly, softly, waiting, while the horse snorted, shook his head and shuffled in the straw. Martha watched, fascinated, and saw Pablo at last venturing forward. He halted as Jess raised a hand slowly.

'That's it. Come along, Pablo.' And the next minute she was fondling his head and ears, still murmuring to him. Presently she slipped a halter about his neck, and brought him docilely out of the stable.

'You've got some sort of magic, you must have,' breathed Martha.

'Let me have him for a while, Martha. He needs a lot of patience and careful treatment. He's only young yet and for some reason highly-strung, a nervous strain in him.'

'We're in your debt already — '

'The horse needs care at once, we mustn't delay, and I've got more space and opportunity than you have at present.' Jess gave the rope to Richard.

'Here, Richard, I want you to lead him gently over to Hilltops at once. Why don't you come back with me now, Martha, and have a look round the place?' she added, as Pablo, still with a brief touch of confidence, allowed Richard to lead him away towards the moors and the other farm.

'I'd like to, thanks Jess. I'll just let Joe know where I am going.'

'I'll tell him, Aunt Martha,' said Penny. 'He's up in the milking-shed.'

'I can't get used to that child speaking,' said Martha, as the two women left the yard, leading Belle.

'Child!' Jess laughed. 'When will you let her grow up, Martha?'

'Yes, it's so silly, isn't it? It must have been with her seeming so helpless — we never realised.'

A few minutes later Jess asked, 'Do you never ride, Martha?'

'Only a little, I've never had the time.' Martha hesitated. 'It's odd. Though I'll do anything for the horses I've always been a bit nervous at the thought of riding.'

'You'll have to get over that, especially if you mean to rear more. They need endless exercise, and your nervousness will communicate itself to the horse. You'll have to get some stable-lads later, too. Start by getting those twins interested. They're just the type. Hardy, light-weight, good-tempered. Come on, get up on Belle now. Make a start.'

Rather clumsily, Martha obeyed, and the horse walked sedately on, Jess holding the reins. The latter grinned up at her. 'Nice, eh?'

Martha's grim look relaxed. 'You're right, Jess, I'll have to get used to this.' After a moment she said, 'Joe will simply *have* to get a housekeeper now when Clare goes. He'll never get me full-time in the house again.'

'You've someone in mind?'

A smile flickered across Martha's face. 'Just about. It's up to Joe.'

14

By the beginning of December Moor-lands Farm was beginning to have a fresh look, straightened up and repaired, a business-like look. Even the extra stables that Martha wanted had begun to take shape, with bargains in building materials that Richard had told them about. Though Joseph was still stern and cool, the enmity with Hilltops was at an end. Only Timothy kept his distance.

'I've nothing to say. Just leave me out of it,' he would say if anything concerning the Laytons cropped up.

One morning, when Johnny and Jimmy arrived for work, their first thought, contrary to custom, was for Clare. They knocked and entered the warm kitchen. Joseph and Martha were busy in the yard somewhere, Penny was setting the breakfast table, and Timothy was rocking in his chair by the red fire, chewing a crust he had stolen off a plate. An appetising smell of bacon filled the air.

'What? Hungry already?' he asked, as the boys came in.

'Nay, we've had breakfast, Mr. Timothy,' said Johnny.

'We want to see Miss Clare,' said Jimmy.

Timothy nodded towards the back kitchen. 'In there. She'll give you a bite o' something if you could do with more.'

'We've got our work to do, Mr. Timothy,' they said together.

They went into the other room and closed the door. Surprised, Clare looked up from a pan of gently sizzling bacon.

'We have an urgent message for you,' began Johnny.

'From Mrs. Walters,' said the other.

'She wants to see you at once.'

'Please will you call at her house as soon as possible, she says.'

'Oh dear, whatever is the matter?' gasped Clare, astonished. Dora had appeared to be so lively and in the best of health recently, and she often called at the farm, helping them as much as she was able. To Clare's pleasure she seemed to be slipping into Moorlands as she herself had done. 'Is she ill?'

'Oh no, Miss Clare. She just wants you to call. She'll be there all day, she says.'

'Won't Mr. Joseph do?'

'No, miss. Mrs. Walters said she must see you special.'

'Private,' put in Jimmy.

'All right, boys. I'll go as soon as I can.'

As she hurried on with her work, Clare puzzled all morning about what it could be Dora wanted that Joseph or somebody else couldn't achieve as well as herself. As soon as dinner was over she got into her car and ran down to Lambreck. Dora welcomed her with a wide smile, so with relief Clare realised it could not be anything really serious.

'Come in, Clare. I want to show you something. They don't get a daily newspaper at Moorlands, do they?'

'No, we rarely see one.' Alarm showed in Clare's face. Newspapers! Surely the horror wasn't starting up again?

'I only get one occasionally, too, but I thought I'd let you know before anyone else did. Look at this!'

She spread out a page of the newspaper and Clare found herself staring down at her own photograph. '*Has Anyone Seen This Woman?*' the headline declared, and underneath: '*Miss Clare Durban missing since early March this year. If anyone knows the whereabouts of Miss Durban, who has perhaps been abroad, please get in touch with Mr. Hugh Jessop, Solicitor, or ask her to do so. She will hear something to her advantage.*'

Clare's finger rested on the one vital word 'advantage', hot blood beating in her cheeks. Dora's voice came as through a mist.

'I thought perhaps you wouldn't want them to know at the farm. It looks like private business.'

'Thanks, Dora. Thank you for letting me know.'

'Well, I mean — ' Dora was puzzled by her stunned look. 'It looked like something important to me. I hope it hasn't given you a shock.'

'I don't know what to make of it — out of the blue like this.' Clare took a deep breath, pulling herself together. Evidently Dora had no idea of what had brought Clare to this part of the country, the trouble that dragged at her heels. She could not have seen those earlier damning papers. 'Mr. Jessop was my father's solicitor.'

'I hope it's good news — ' but Dora still sounded doubtful. Clare looked far from happy, the colour now drained from her face, leaving her pale and sickly-looking.

'It might be — ' Clare shook her head, terribly afraid. Was it genuine — or was it a hoax? A nasty trick, someone trying to hound her down again? 'Dora, I'd like to ask Richard's advice. Can I cut this out and show him?'

'Take the whole paper. Clare, if I'd kept quiet about it, someone else might have noticed it.'

'You did right to let me know. I'm grateful, Dora. Don't worry about it. I left my home in the south because I was unhappy there, friendless — and when I found this place, I've been so happy here, Dora. I don't want anything to destroy this happiness. I don't want to be dragged back.'

'Well, I *hope* I've done right,' said Dora. 'We all like you so much, Clare. I wouldn't like to spoil things for you.'

Clare drove over to find Richard at once. He was helping Jess in the stables and showed his surprise as his fiancée came looking for him.

'You're early today, Clare,' he said. 'I'm not free yet. I like to do as much as I can for Jess till her arm is really strong.'

'I can wait. Something has turned up, and I want your advice — to talk about it.'

Seeing her worried face he swung around, water spilling from the pail he carried. 'What is it, darling? If someone has been making trouble for you again — '

'I don't think it's trouble — at least I hope not.' She held out the newspaper with it folded and showing her photograph. 'Dora Walters saw this and sent for me.'

'We don't have this paper and it's evening before we ever get a chance to read.' He scanned the announcement quickly, his brows puckered.

As he looked up at her she said, 'Do you think it's a hoax, Richard? I don't know whether to get in touch with Mr. Jessop or keep quiet. Perhaps no one else will have noticed this. I couldn't bear it to start all over again, ruining our happiness together.'

'It can never do that, Clare darling. Nothing is going to come between us.'

'Or do you think — is it possible they've found something to clear my name?'

'Could be. Do you know this Mr. Jessop?'

'Of course, very well. He was my father's solicitor, and I'm sure he at least knew how much of my life I gave up to my uncle, reading to him, writing his letters, doing errands, playing cards and draughts with him when he was well enough. Mr. Jessop is a kind, patient man, and he knew I was a good companion for Uncle Ronald, that I would never hurt him.'

'Then I see no harm in paying him a visit. I'll go down with you. We'll do this together, Clare. Go into the house and phone, my dear — make an appointment for tomorrow afternoon if possible. We'll get off early in the morning.'

Clare left Richard to his work and called in to see Mrs. Layton, asking to use the telephone. When she got through to Mr. Jessop's office, he was not there, but she spoke to his secretary and made an appointment for late afternoon next day.

When she went back to tell Richard, he said, 'Fine! Better than wondering and fretting about it. We'll go in your car, Clare, then if you find you have to stay, I'll get a late train back.'

'It is good of you, Richard. I feel much better with you helping me. I'll run back to Dora's and ask her to help them out at Moorlands while I am away.'

'I'll do as much as I can today and warn Stephen and Malcolm that I'll be having time off. We'll leave at eight o'clock or even earlier if you like.'

'Earlier, Richard. I'll be awake having this on my mind.'

'Don't worry about it, my dear. It sounds promising to me.' He smiled at her encouragingly, longing to wipe the strain from her pretty face for good.

She showed the newspaper to Joseph so that he wouldn't be alarmed at her leaving suddenly and could explain to the others. Dora had promised only too willingly to come up in her place while she was away. It was still dark when she backed the car out into the yard the following morning. Joseph was already up and having a quick snack before going out to start work, and he stood at the gateway to watch her drive off.

'I'll be back, Joseph,' she called. 'I'll be back as soon as possible.'

Richard saw her headlamps and came out immediately to join her. 'You drive, Richard,' she said, sliding across to the other seat. 'You know these lanes in the dark better than I do. I'll take over later if you want.'

They had lunch somewhere in the south Midlands then set off on the remaining part of the journey. 'What are you smiling at?' asked Richard as they left the restaurant.

'I was just wondering how Dora was coping with the farm's big dinner.'

Richard laughed. 'I'll put my bet on Dora. She'll win through.'

They talked for a while about the little cottage they were having renovated for their future life together. It was an enchanting place, nestling amongst trees and flowers, with a large garden and built with artistic, fascinating angles. Clare had been delighted with it when Richard took her to see it. Except for that they had not talked much on the way down, but it did not need continual conversation to keep them happy with each other. They drove into Clare's old home town in plenty of time for refreshments and a brush-up before her appointment.

Mr. Jessop's office was in a narrow, dingy street and up narrow stairs covered in brown linoleum. Once inside the door bearing the solicitor's name, however, things looked brighter. Clean polished wood, leather chairs and red mats, and windows to let the sunshine in whenever there was any. The secretary who had spoken to her on the telephone apparently was new there, a stranger to Clare.

Mr. Jessop saw her at once. He rose from his wide, leather-topped, paper-littered desk and held out his hand. An elderly man with long, thick white hair and aristocratic features, who had known her from childhood.

'I'm so glad you've come, Clare,' he said, his voice warm and friendly. 'I've been searching in every likely place for you without success. So we had to have the assistance of the Press. You didn't go abroad, did you?'

She shook her head. 'No.'

'I always had my doubts about that — something you said once, and I knew you'd always had a hankering for Scotland.'

Clare watched him anxiously. So she hadn't been as clever as she thought! He had always thought he could get hold of her when he wanted her. 'Sit down, my dear,' he said gently. She sat on the edge of the chair by the side of the desk, while he turned over several papers in front of him.

'First of all I must tell you that Mrs.

Staines, your uncle's old nurse, has died.'

Clare's hands clenched. Was that all? Had she travelled down here simply to hear of the death of the woman she detested, who had said such vile things about her?

'So the house and everything in it is now yours.' As Clare was miserably silent, he went on, 'Before she died she sent for me and told me the truth of your uncle's death. She has cleared your name at last.'

Clare bent forward, her eyes brightening. Mr. Jessop went on, 'Your uncle had bouts of terrible pain, as you know, Clare. It must have become unbearable at times. That night when Mrs. Staines had to visit a relative who was sick, he begged her to bring the bottle of tablets and leave it with him. He had begged her many a time to give him more. After you had taken his drink he swallowed nearly all those tablets. Clare, your uncle committed suicide.'

She drew a deep long breath. 'At last!

At last I am free of all those ugly suspicions.'

'Yes, and I'll see that it is made public, of course. You have suffered enough. I don't think Mrs. Staines thought he would take so many. She did all she could not to have his name blackened.'

'It didn't matter about mine,' said Clare bitterly.

'She was always jealous of you. It was spite, I suppose, but when she was taken ill and knew it was the end — she wanted to clear her conscience.' He put a ring of keys on the desk. 'Here are the keys to the house.'

Clare sat up straight. 'I want you to sell the house — and the contents. I don't want it. I have found a new home.'

'There might be a few things you'd like to keep,' he said patiently. 'Go and have a look over it. After that I will see to everything for you.'

'I suppose I ought to see it once more. Was Mrs. Staines — did she die there?'

'She died in hospital. Collect anything you want then leave it to me. Leave your new address — '

'I'm going to be married. I'm staying up in the north.'

'That's good news.' Mr. Jessop smiled at her with relief. 'I'm so glad it is all straightened out. I often worried about you.'

'It will be hard to forget — some things,' said Clare, rising and picking up her gloves.

'I know, but try to put it behind you.'

'I'm grateful for all you have done for me, Mr. Jessop. You helped to set me free.' Clare wrote the address of Moorlands on a piece of paper and handed it to him. 'That address will always find me. I'll drop the keys in tomorrow.'

'Take your time at the house. I don't want you to regret anything.'

She met his gaze steadily. 'There is nothing to regret in that life, Mr. Jessop.'

She went out to Richard, who was

waiting in the car for her, her face alight with happiness. She snuggled up against him.

'Richard, it's all right! I'm free — I can prove my innocence at last. It matters that I can prove it to you more than anybody.' Briefly she told him of what had happened.

'I always knew you spoke the truth, my darling. I couldn't have loved you otherwise.'

'You helped so much believing me — so that — ' she fell silent as, his arms about her, he kissed her hard on the lips, regardless of amused passers-by, and what words she had been about to say were never uttered.

They walked about the town, did a little shopping and had a meal before Richard left by train for the north. Clare had booked a room for the night at a small hotel, as she had no intention of going back to her uncle's house till daylight.

After breakfast next day she went over to the tall old house in the suburbs. It looked just as gloomy as ever as she sat a moment in the car, staring up at it. A woman passed, gazing at her then abruptly turning away. A familiar figure living in this road who had no doubt been one to throw mud at her, but what did it matter now? She detested them all and would never see them again. Pulling herself together, she got out and went up the untidy path and unlocked the brown door. She shivered as dampish cold air met her in the dim hall.

Leaving the door open to the frosty morning she walked into the front, high-ceilinged sitting-room and began a systematic search from room to room. Turning over the contents of drawers and cupboards, finding little of value amongst the plain, old-fashioned objects. The kitchen and other parts of the house had been left dusty and untidy, as though the last occupant had left in a hurry. Evidently Mrs. Staines had been taken ill suddenly and taken away, and no one had cared enough to clean up after her. Clare looked at soiled pots and pans in the sink, at the rumpled tablecloth and some mouldy bread with distaste, but she could not bring herself to touch them. She couldn't get away from this house, with its foul memories quick enough.

It took all her nerve to enter her uncle's bedroom. It had not been used and the bare mattress and the furniture without Uncle Ronald's bottles, books and toilet articles, was saddening. Even the drawers were empty. Mrs. Staines had got rid of all his belongings there and wiped that room clean. Clare shut the door upon it firmly, got two suitcases from a cupboard and filled them with a few books and objects she and her uncle had treasured, and took them to the car. The door to the house locked once more, she hoped that would be the last time she would look on its unwelcoming façade and its long, neglected garden.

After something to eat she dropped the keys in at Mr. Jessop's office. He had not yet returned for the afternoon. 'Please tell Mr. Jessop that I've finished at my uncle's house,' she said to his secretary. She turned to go, then paused. 'You might tell him, too, please, that the house is rather disordered. He might like to send a woman in to clean up a bit before he disposes of anything. He understands my wishes.'

She walked away feeling light as air. This must be, indeed, the end to that awful phase of her life. It was growing dark but she headed northwards, eager to leave this place behind her once and for all. At the garage where she stopped for petrol the man warned her to be careful, the roads were icy.

'I'll be careful,' she promised, but nothing was going to prevent her driving on. She did not care whatever time she got there so long as she reached the surroundings she now thought of as home. As she had promised she took care and took her time, but always edging nearer her beloved moors, and sometime in the frosty, moonlight night she arrived. Only the dogs were there to greet her, Laddie nearly knocking her over with his boisterous welcome, and only then did she remember the bolted kitchen door. She would have to stay in the car, then. Tentatively she tried the latch and to her surprise the door opened and, in the moonlight streaming through the uncurtained window, Sam lifted his head. He came over to welcome her in as the other dogs had done, only in a much more sober, stately manner, while she softly closed and fastened the door. So they had been expecting her! Probably Richard had warned them that she was not staying away and would be back at any hour.

She crept up to her room and managed to snatch a few hours sleep. When Joseph came down in the morning the kettle was already bubbling on the hob and Clare was setting the table. She smiled at him cheerfully as he entered the kitchen.

Speechless for a moment, his face

brightening, he suddenly strode out to the hall and yelled up the stairs, 'Hurry up, everybody! She's back!'

'You didn't really think I could keep away, did you?' Clare teased him.

They all came down at once to see her, happy and relieved, as though they had doubted whether she would really return to them, even old Timothy struggling into his clothes, still only half-dressed.

'Didn't I tell you?' he gloated. 'She was bound to come back. She belongs to us.'

'Dora will be here soon,' said Martha, with a sly glance at her brother, as they sat at breakfast.

'So soon?' exclaimed Clare, surprised. Dora had certainly not wasted much time, digging herself into Moorlands.

'I've hardly had to do a thing,' said Martha. 'She's been great.'

'I'm glad, because I shall be leaving soon to get married, and if you will let Dora take my place — '

'She'll take your place all right!' laughed Martha. 'Come on, Joe, speak up!'

'Yes,' he said solemnly. 'Dora and I are going to get married.'

Clare smiled delightedly. 'That's marvellous news. I'm so happy for you, Joseph.'

'And I'll be getting married someday soon, too,' put in Penny.

'Aye,' said old Timothy, rising and looking for his pipe. 'Wedding bells all round. Perhaps it's the best thing for all of you, after all. We only have to get Martha fixed up now.'

'Oh no, you won't!' declared Martha. 'I won't leave my animals for any man. I'm fine as I am.'

'I couldn't picture you anywhere else but in the yard at Moorlands, Martha,' laughed Clare, rising. 'Now, if you will excuse me, I must leave you for a short time. I have a date at Hilltops.' She laughed at a grumbling murmur from Timothy and patted his scanty-haired head as she passed. 'And nothing you can say, Mr. Timothy, will stop me marrying Richard Layton.'

She stepped briskly down the glistening, frosty road, with Laddie loping along in front. The morning was still not quite clear, but a light beckoned across from Hilltops as she turned into the lane leading up there, as though Richard were there waiting. He would be expecting her, listening for her step. He would know she would fly back to his arms as straight as an arrow. No more fears and suspicions, nothing to keep them apart any more . . . back to Richard where she truly belonged.

THE END

ACCIDENT PRONE

Anna Ramsay

From hospital ward sister to sanatorium sister at Ditchingham Prep School is a drastic change, but Ruth Silke needs something different. Working with Dr Daniel Gather, the local GP who covers the school, isn't so easy — particularly when he seems all too matter-of-fact about his young son Danny, a boarder at the school. Ruth is convinced that Danny's accidents are a cry for help, but how to persuade Dan? Particularly when their own relationship leaves so much to be desired . . .